THE HERA WARS

by

Edward O. Bast

© Copyright 2007, Ed Bast

All Rights Reserved.

No part of this book may be reproduced, stored in a retrieval system, or transmitted by any means, electronic, mechanical, photocopying, recording, or otherwise, without written permission from the author.

This is a work of fiction. Names, characters, places and incidents either are the product of the author's imagination or are used fictitiously, and any resemblance to any actual persons, living or dead, events or locales is entirely coincidental.

ISBN: 978-1-60388-999-5
(1-60388-999-X)

For Christopher

PROLOGUE

The 14th Terrestrial Division had just occupied a small planet in the G061355 System over 250 light years from earth. As part of the III Intergalactic Corps of the 5th Frontier Fleet of Space Command, its mission was to establish a base of operations on the planet and explore it for human habitation. The 5th Frontier Fleet would then occupy the planet, help establish the new civilization, and maintain marshal law until such time as the new civilization could take hold and form its own governing and defensive body. This procedure had been successfully carried out on other systems, but never so deep in space. But with an exploding human population, exasperated by the proven scientific capability of extending the span of human life several fold, it was the determination of the world governing body, C.O.P.E. (Confederation of Planet Earth), to preserve the Race by scattering it to the very corners of the universe.

The 14th Terrestrial Division was comprised primarily of research and engineering units, but was not unarmed. Although life had long ago been discovered on other planets and moons in other systems, no intelligent forms had yet been found. Of all life yet known, ranging any where from a simple virus to elaborate species, humans still reigned supreme in each new terrestrial home they discovered or inhabited. But C.O.P.E. elected not to take any chances. Extra-terrestrial life was no longer questioned and was considered old news in the dozen or so places that man had extended his boundaries. The remaining question that still nagged the imagination of the species was, were we the only ones capable of creating instruments of death and destruction? C.O.P.E. chose the safest and most logical route. If there was intelligent life out there capable of and of the mind to attack the

Race, we should not allow ourselves to be unprepared and lose everything we have worked so hard to preserve. The Race should not only be capable of defending itself, but should also have the offensive capability to close with and destroy an invading force.

The III Intergalactic Corps was the spearhead of the 5th Frontier Fleet and occupied the larger than Mars-size planet in true military fashion. After searching for any intelligent life through various instruments of the radio, light, and temperature spectrums at a safe and unobtrusive distance from the planet, probes are sent in to determine the life supporting characteristics of the prospective orb. When the planet appears inhabitable, an armed division with the appropriate research and construction capability is sent in to secure and establish a landing base and reconnoiter the immediate area for any hazards that might hinder the arrival and future operations of the remainder of the corps. Once III Intergalactic Corps is established, 5th Frontier Fleet will send in the rest of the corps to establish other prime locations around the planet for the introduction of the civilian transports accompanying the fleet. This is actually a quick process that requires only a matter of weeks. Establishing the civilian infrastructure for permanent residence on the planet can take several years. Additionally, the planet would not be able to support the large contingent of the Race arriving all at once, so 5th Frontier Fleet, particularly many of the civilian transports and a multitude of supply ships constituting several relatively small convoys spread over great distances and soaring rapidly through space, would arrive at the new planet at specific intervals. Like the head and fangs of a great serpent, the bulk of the military contingent leads the grand odyssey to its new home. The remainder of the military contingent serves as escorts for the smaller convoys stretched out through space. Each frontier fleet that snakes its way through the black void to plant the seed of human existence on distant worlds is truly the greatest and most spectacular feat of mankind's relatively short history.

CHAPTER ONE

Major General Gregory Swanson lay on his small aluminum and canvas cot; his left arm curled up underneath his weary head for support, and puffed on a well-deserved cigarette. The light blue-gray smoke floated effortlessly to the off-white ceiling of the twelve foot by fourteen foot cubical he called home. He didn't need much space. Just enough for the cot, his wooden field desk with folding chair, a footlocker, and a metal wall locker for his clothes was all the space he required. Situated in the Command Module of the 14th Terrestrial Division Headquarters, MG. Gregory Swanson, a forty-five year veteran, was seldom far from his Command Post (CP). His long and distinguished service in Space Command had won him this sought-after opportunity of spearheading this migration, dubbed Operation Homestead, to its new home. With his entire division now safely on the new planet named Hera; after the ancient Greek queen of heaven, the wife and sister of Zeus, MG. Swanson could finally lay back on his cot for a short rest.

Staring up at the ceiling, Swanson watched as the ghost-like smoke climbed away from him. He thought of nothing. It was a conscious effort for such a man of details to try to think of nothing. When he was reminded of some particular of the mission, he'd abruptly shake his head to the side, first left then back to the right, one time, to clear the thought from his mind. MG. Swanson stretched the tightness from his long limbs, his tall frame taking up every inch of the six-foot cot. He coughed lightly and remembered the advice from the Division Surgeon that he should give up tobacco. Smoking was one of those physiological idiosyncrasies of man's character. Science had found it easier to cure the diseases of man than to break him of his bad habits.

Smoking may have been one of Swanson's bad habits, but overlooking details was not. The operation was going just as planned. His combat brigades, the 1st and 2nd Light Combat Brigades, were deployed in positions around the perimeter of the large base of operations. Although C.O.P.E. had never run into any intelligent threat in its decades of deep space exploration, they always went prepared in the event of unforeseen trouble. Where they were, they could not be reinforced. However now, with no enemies except what nature might throw at them, the combat brigades served mostly as sentinels ensuring that no one wandered off and got hurt. The construction brigades, the bulk of the division, were busy making permanent facilities for the division and the other arriving units of III Corps, and the research unit was gathering environmental and life systems data within the perimeter. Swanson let out a long sigh, crushed out his cigarette and drifted to sleep.

Sometime later there came a knock at the door. Swanson sat up with a jerk in his cot, the mist of sleep clouding his mind so that, for a brief moment, he wasn't sure where he was.

"Enter," he said finally, rubbing the sleep from his eyes.

The cubical door slid open. Standing at the threshold was Colonel Satake, his G3 (Operations) Officer.

"What is it, Yuchi?" Swanson said through a stifled yawn.

"Sir, you really need to come see this."

Normally, Gregory Swanson would have requested more information, but there was a sense of urgency in the colonel's voice that made Swanson realize that action was required more at this point than explanation. He had known Col. Yuchi Satake for many years, and the capable Japanese officer was the epitome of professionalism and not easily swayed by trivial matters. That's why Gregory chose Satake to be his G3 for this mission.

Swanson sprung out of bed and followed Yuchi down the narrow corridor of the command module that led to the

Operations Center. As they proceeded towards the Ops Center, Col. Satake quickly updated the General.

"Long Range Imagery picked up a moving object some five or six million k's (kilometers) away, closing at an extremely high rate of speed. Suddenly the object disappeared and reappeared instantaneously three million k's away but in a different quadrant. Computer calculations put its lateral shift, if you can believe this, at about sixty times the speed of light. Then it disappeared again and reappeared in another quadrant 180 degrees from its first shift. This time the computer registered the speed of the object as being twice as fast as before."

Gregory Swanson shook his head. "Are you sure it's the same object."

"Pretty sure," Satake replied. "Spectrum analysis seems to confirm it. But the strangest thing is its lateral jumps. The object appears to be closing in on us, but most of its movements are back and forth and in no particular pattern."

"Where's General Wilson?"

"She's in the Ops Center, Sir. She's been briefed."

As they entered the Ops Center, someone called 'CG (Commanding General) on station' to alert the staff that MG. Swanson was present. Brigadier General Beverly Wilson turned from the computer screen that she and Major Tom Crawford were watching and greeted her commanding officer.

"Good afternoon, Sir," BG. Wilson sighed, showing a sense of relief that her commander was there to take over.

"What have we got, Bev?" Swanson asked as he searched the large brown eyes of his executive officer. BG. Beverly Wilson was a tall, attractive black woman who had served in uniform for the last twenty-nine years. A product of the Race's migration into space, Beverly was born and raised on Mars, but immigrated to earth in order to join Space Command. Also hand picked by MG. Swanson, Beverly Wilson was a seasoned space traveler who had served under him before. She was one of the few who could boast that she had spent more time aboard ship than most of her counterparts. But today, her normally smiling eyes were dulled by her anxiety.

"I don't know, Greg," she replied putting her long, slender fingers up to her neck. "It's the damnedest thing I've ever seen." Beverly quickly briefed the general in an efficient military style, and although she remained professional as always, Swanson noticed more nervous gestures than he had ever seen when she was in uniform. Perhaps, he thought, the situation had rattled off a bit of her professional armor allowing the true woman inside to shine through.

"Have we contacted Corps yet, Bev?" Swanson asked.

"No, Sir. I wanted to brief you first."

Swanson turned to Col. Satake. "Okay. Let's get Corps G3 on the horn. I want to apprise them of this. And Yuchi, make sure all the data, everything, is piped to III Corps. Leave nothing out."

"Yes, Sir." Col. Satake nodded.

"And when we get Corps G3 on the horn, patch it into my office. I'll take it there. And keep me posted on the status of that thing."

"Yes, Sir."

Swanson turned back to BG. Wilson. "Bev, come with me in my office."

"Yes, sir," Wilson replied, her confidence back in her voice.

The two generals walked across the large Operations Center through the maze of field desks and computer terminals to Swanson's office at the far corner. As they entered the office, Greg Swanson closed the door behind Beverly Wilson and asked her to sit down.

"You want some coffee, Bev?"

Beverly's eyes smiled at last. "That would be great," she sighed.

Swanson made two cups of instant coffee and handed Wilson a cup and sat down in the chair next to her. As he lit a cigarette, he looked deep into her eyes as if searching for her mind's thoughts. "What do you think that thing is out there, Bev?"

"Oh, Greg, I don't know." Wilson bit on her lower lip and gazed momentarily into her cup. "Of all my years in space," she continued, "I've never seen anything like it."

"Do you think it's fabricated?"

Beverly looked straight into Greg's green eyes, her own brown eyes full of innocent fear. "I don't think it's natural."

"Then it would have to be intelligent, wouldn't it?"

BG. Beverly Wilson did not reply. They both knew the possible consequences of that.

The phone rang on the small, metal desk and Swanson got up and answered it. "General Swanson. Okay, put him through." Greg sat down at his desk, crushed out his cigarette, and turned on the small monitor that sat to one corner of the desktop. Shortly the image of Colonel Steinfeld came on the screen. "Good day, Heinrich," Swanson said flatly.

Swanson waited for the signal to travel to the III Corps Command Ship and for Col. Steinfeld's reply. The great distance of the ship from the planet, Hera, required time for the signals to go back and forth, even with the use of the signal accelerator.

"Good day, Sir. How's everything on Hera?"

"Heinrich, I have a situation. The CG needs to be briefed. Now listen carefully." After Swanson explained the phenomena to Col. Steinfeld, he lit another cigarette and sipped on his cup of coffee. As he waited for the reply, Swanson turned to Beverly Wilson, who had been sitting patiently in her chair. "Bev, this may be a little premature, but I want you to go and alert the brigades."

Aboard the III Intergalactic Corps Command Ship, Earth ship *Bangkok*, Lieutenant General Robert (Bob) Eastman stared at the communications monitor as he waited for MG. Swanson's reply to come back from Hera. Eastman and Swanson were classmates at the C.O.P.E. Army Officers Basic Course in Frankfurt and had chased each other up the career ladder over the past few decades to their current positions. Despite the vast kilometers apart their separate career progressions had taken them, they had always remained in touch and helped each other whenever they could. They were the closest of friends.

Swanson's image finally appeared on the screen. He looked somber and somewhat tired from the past two hours of constant communication between Hera and the Earth ship *Bangkok*.

"Well, Bob," Greg Swanson began. "The object continues to make progress towards Hera. We can no longer track all of its lateral movements because Hera's rotation is taking us out of full field of view. I have moved Earth ship *Ottawa* (14th Terrestrial Division's mother ship) out of her geocentric orbit with Base Ops and am placing her in a longitudinal orbit around the poles that will afford us continuous monitoring of the phenomena. However this will mean periodic breaks in communication with her from here when we lose line-of-sight of her during segments of her orbit. We are going to have daybreak here shortly, and I've gone ahead and placed the Division on full alert and issued the rules of engagement that you directed. We will not open fire unless human life is threatened, and we will use the minimum force necessary to negate any threat.

"To answer you questions," MG. Swanson continued. "It would take us approximately seventy-two hours to reload all personnel and minimal equipment and stores onto the shuttles and supply ships and link back up with Earth ship *Ottawa* and begin our return back to Fleet. It would take approximately two weeks to break down the operation in its entirety.

"Not knowing the threat, or if it even is a threat, it is impossible at this point to estimate how long we could hold out if attacked before III Corps would arrive within striking distance.

"Bob, I got to tell you," Swanson sighed. "We are getting a bit antsy down here. Although it has posed no apparent threat so far, this thing is just too strange to ignore. When we set up, I placed the Division in a location that was easily defendable from the ground, yet large enough to support Base Operations and the landing of the other divisions. But we are pretty vulnerable from the air. Knowing that there was nothing on Hera to pose such a threat, air defense was not at the top of our priority list. How could we know that something might come at us from outer space?

"Anyway, we'll keep you abreast of the situation and continue to send you all the data we collect on this thing. End of transmission."

LG. Bob Eastman ran his knuckle back and forth across his lips as he stared at the blank screen from which the image of his friend, Greg Swanson, had just disappeared. He looked up at Col. Steinfeld, who had been standing across from him during Swanson's transmission. "Any word yet from Fleet?"

"No, sir," Steinfeld shook his head. "But Comms confirms that they are receiving the data we are sending them."

"They must be thinking," Eastman grunted, placing his head in his hands. "How far out are we now from Hera?"

"About five days out at our current speed."

Suddenly the watch officer ran up to LG. Eastman and Col. Steinfeld. "Sir, the 14th's data signal is breaking up. And Comms reports that they can no longer raise Hera through the signal accelerator."

"Anything from Fleet?" Steinfeld asked.

"No, Sir. Nothing," the major replied.

"Damn it," Eastman burst. "I'm not going to wait for them any longer. Get me Admiral Rodriguez on the horn."

"Yes, sir," the watch officer replied, turning on his heels to go and raise the commander of the III Corps escort fleet.

The escort fleet comprised of a Bremen-class carrier (Earth ship *Singapore*) containing sixty-four fighter-bombers capable of operations in space as well as in atmospheric conditions. Swift and agile, these three-man crewed aircraft were designed to provide protection for the fleet as well as air support for ground operations. Four Hiroshima-class battle cruisers accompanied the carrier. As a small part of the 5th Frontier Fleet's entire defensive capability, they were designed to be disassembled while in orbit at Hera and reassembled as part of a larger oceangoing fleet on Hera. This was to be the fate of most spacecraft within the Fleet; only a portion of the Fleet, the worm-hole capable vessels and a major part of the military contingent, would return to the solar system via a wormhole for further service in Space Command. Most ships and people therein would remain on Hera forever and become the new foundation for this arm of the Race.

When Admiral Rodriguez came on the monitor, LG. Eastman sat down to talk to him.

"Tony, have you been monitoring communication with the 14th?" LG. Eastman and Admiral Anthony Rodriguez had not met before the assembly of 5th Frontier Fleet for this mission, but they hit it off right from the start and worked very well together.

"Yeah, Bob," Rodriguez replied, "but we lost contact a few minutes ago." Because of Corps' and the escort fleet's close proximity to each other, communications was instantaneous.

"Tony, their situation down there has me concerned," Eastman continued. "Nothing like this has ever happened before, and since we are in unfamiliar territory, I don't want to take any chances. Whatever it is out there, it's nothing we have ever encountered in nature, so I have to assume, for the welfare of everyone concerned, that it isn't natural."

"What does Fleet advise?" Rodriguez asked.

"They haven't responded yet. But I want to at least get us in a position to assist the 14th if that becomes necessary." Eastman paused for a moment. "How fast can your fighters get to Hera and how long can they remain on station once there?"

"Whew," Rodriguez let out a heavy breath. "At this range and at max speed, I guess they could be there in a day or so. But once there, they couldn't remain on station very long without refueling."

"How long?"

"Well, if they remain in space maybe an hour or so. But if they need to combat operate under atmospheric conditions, hmm, probably only a few minutes."

Bob Eastman hesitated but a moment before issuing his next command. "Tony, I would like you and two of your battle cruisers to move out at flank speed for Hera. As soon as you get close enough that your fighters can stay on station for twenty minutes at sea level, I want you to launch a Flight at full speed towards the 14th..."

"You haven't cleared this with Fleet, have you?" the Admiral interrupted.

"Tony, no, I haven't," Eastman sighed.

"Why don't we send the armed drones, Bob?" Rodriguez suggested. "Fleet can't bitch at that."

"No, I've thought of that, Tony. We have friendlies on the ground. I want humans making the decisions there; not robots."

LG. Eastman paused. "But I promise you, if any bullets fly, I'll take the hit."

Rodriguez chuckled. "Hell, Bob, if any bullets fly, I'm sure there will be enough to go around for the both of us? Anything else?" Tony Rodriguez was a tall, husky, straight shooting Naval Officer who normally wouldn't take a leak without guidance from Fleet, but he was a professional who understood the possible gravity of the situation and well understood that inaction in the face of the absence of orders could be worse than displaying an aggressive initiative.

"Yeah, while at flank speed, launch three Flights at fifteen minute intervals. Anything after that is at your discretion."

"What's my weapons' status?" Rodriguez asked, referring to whether or not his fighters could fire.

"Weapons Hold," Eastman replied. "But if there are any aggressive actions against the Flight or the 14th, your fighters can go to Weapons Free at their discretion."

"Aye, aye, sir," Rodriguez sighed. "I'll be taking the *Boston* and the *Hiroshima* with me. I'll leave you the *Saõ Paulo* and the *Milan*. We'll be departing at flank speed in about ten minutes. Anything else, Bob?"

"No, Tony. Good luck."

LG. Swanson turned from the monitor screen and instructed that one of the ship's external cameras be focused on the carrier, Earth ship *Singapore,* and the image be placed on the large screen in the Operations Center. He watched as the large, beautiful, arrowhead-shaped carrier gracefully slipped out of convoy formation and maneuvered into launch position with the battle cruisers, Earth ships *Boston* and *Hiroshima*. At twenty-nine stories at the thickest part of its tapered body and at over 800 meters long, the Earth ship *Singapore* was one of the largest ships in the fleet and a very impressive sight to behold. The two identical, cigar-shaped battle cruisers were much smaller at only

15 stories high and around 400 meters long. Swanson thought about the excitement and anticipation that there must have been on the three ships, especially with the gun crews that had to date only fired their pulse-laser guns during target practice and at errant asteroids.

As LG. Eastman watched the three ships line up to speed towards Hera, Col. Steinfeld rushed to his side.

"Sir, we lost all contact with the 14th."

Robert Eastman didn't even turn his head. He just stared at the three large vessels of war preparing for their flight.

"Sir," Steinfeld continued. "The last thing we received was Morse over the data net. Sir, they said that the stars were disappearing."

Robert Eastman watched as the three ships moved swiftly ahead of the convoy, their speed ever increasing, until momentarily they zipped out of sight.

"Hang in there, Greg," The General whispered as he stared out into deep space after the Earth ship *Singapore* and her escorts. "We're on our way."

CHAPTER TWO

Aboard the Earth ship *Singapore*, Adm. Rodriguez stared at the outboard camera monitor as the colorful collage of warped light caused by their tremendous velocity whipped around the ship. Only the two escorting battle cruisers looked normal because of their identical speed. Captain Rita Becker, the ship's captain, approached Rodriguez at the screen.

"We've reached flank speed, Admiral."

"Thanks, Rita," Rodriguez said quietly as he stared at the screen. "Anything else from Hera?"

"No, sir," Becker said flatly as she turned her head towards the screen. "Just that last Morse transmission over the data net before we lost Comms with her." Rita paused a moment. "What do you think they meant, 'The stars are disappearing'?"

Rodriguez shook his head and forced out a sharp quick breath. "Beats the hell out of me, Rita. Well," he turned towards the Captain, "I guess we'll find out soon enough. Have your flight crews been briefed?"

"They're being briefed now on everything we've got...which isn't much. We've got about five hours before we launch the first flight. When do you plan to sound General Quarters for the Task Force?"

"Aw, probably just before launch. Even at the fighters' accelerated speed, they will still have several hours before they reach target. Unless we run into anything screwy before then, of course."

"I talked with the captains aboard the *Boston* and *Hiroshima*; everyone is naturally pretty anxious. They said their crews are actually hoping for a fight. Can you believe it?"

"Yeah," Rodriguez nodded, taking in a deep breath. "It's in our genes. Of course, we don't know what we're facing. They may change their minds pretty damn quick." He shook his head. "Hell, we aren't even sure if this thing isn't some natural phenomenon or, even if it is a superior intelligence, that it's hostile. The fact remains, and our history will bear me out, the only intelligent being we have ever fought was ourselves."

Rita Becker slid her long, slender fingers through her short, red curly hair. "Admiral, I'm going to go to my cabin for a cup of fresh coffee. Would you like to join me?"

"Rita, that's the best idea I've heard here recently. I would love to."

On the way to the Captain's Cabin, the two senior officers stopped at the bridge. The Watch Officer on duty was Commander Beung Hyuk Kim, a handsome man with jet black hair and a pug nose that rested on his large cheekbones. Commander Kim, who could trace his lineage all the way back to ancient Korea, was one of the last few whose ancestry had never married outside of their race, a distinction that Kim wore like a badge of honor.

After the two senior officers were briefed by Kim, they retreated to the Captain's Cabin for a hot cup of coffee. This plush office was where Rita Becker did her administrative work, held conferences with the ship's senior officers, and occasionally sought temporary refuge from the rigors of command. As they entered the cabin, Rita glanced over at her large oaken desk, one of the few furnishings in the entire ship that was made of natural wood. She grimaced at the large stacks of paper work that cluttered her work station. After all the eons of technological advancement, the Race was still clinging on to hard copies; people always felt more comfortable if they could hold something in their hands. But it was different now. 'Paper', as it was still called, no longer came from wood but was made of ashen compounds easily extracted from bodies in space, such as asteroids. It was more durable, lighter, and not as flammable as true paper and could be easily recycled aboard a vessel so equipped.

Captain Becker offered the Admiral a chair at the large oval mahogany conference table. She quickly prepared two cups of coffee, placed them on a tray with an ashtray, and brought them to the table. She chose not to sit at her usual spot at the head of the table, but sat instead in a chair across from her boss. As Rita settled in the chair, she reached into her slacks pocket and pulled out her cigarette case and an electric lighter. Admiral Rodriguez watched in silence as she took a cigarette out of the case, lit it, and took several hard drags before reaching for her cup of coffee. He could feel the stress within her.

"How's your husband, Rita?" Tony Rodriguez finally asked.

"We're getting divorced," she replied flatly and with no apparent emotion.

Tony frowned. "What? Why didn't you tell me? I could have picked someone else for this mission and let you stay back in the System (solar system) to work things out."

"I didn't want to stay in the System, Tony. I'm damn glad you offered me this stint. I needed a change of scenery. Besides," she continued between sips of coffee, "the breakup was mutual. Our careers were taking us further and further apart. No hard feelings. Just 'Auf Wiedersehen' and 'Fare thee well.'"

"Well, hell, Rita, I still wished you would've told me."

"Why?" Rita chuckled. "Then you just would've worried like you're beginning to do right now. Anyway, that's the last thing on my mind. Right now, I'm more concerned about my flight crews that I'm shortly going to send screaming at top speed into God only knows what."

"Don't worry. They're going to come back."

"Yeah, but in how many pieces?"

"Rita, we've been exploring deep space for over five centuries. There has never been any sign of threat other than our own fear riddled imaginations. I'm beginning to believe we are it. The universe is ours."

Rita rubbed her tired green eyes with her long, slender fingers. "Tony, they may not be Navy, but the ground forces on Hera are still good, intelligent people. Why would they report that the stars were disappearing?"

Lieutenant Hans Zimmermann was in the lead fighter-bomber of the first Flight from Earth ship *Singapore*. The delta-winged fighter-bombers carried a crew of three; the pilot, the navigator/bombardier, and the gunner. Nicknamed the Hellcat, it boasted a large triangular-shaped tail and computer-operated retractable wings that could be extended for maneuvering and takeoffs and landings, and retracted for lightning speed. The Hellcat was capable of both atmospheric and space operations, vertical takeoffs and landings, and operations in zero visibility conditions.

The Hellcat had two pulse-laser cannons mounted in bubble-shaped turrets, one on top of the aerospace craft and a second one on the belly. Both were retracted into recesses when not in use. The gunner could man either one from inside the turrets or remotely operate them together or individually from the gunner's station located behind the cockpit. The pulse-laser cannons could be fired manually or computer operated. In the computer operated mode, the gunner would identify and lock on the targets with radar. The computer would then track and fire on the target. In a hostile, target-rich environment, the gunner had the capability to go to the "Weapons-free, Fully Automatic" mode. In this mode, the computer and radar took over all gunnery operations. The radar, which was capable of identifying and tracking three hundred and fifty individual targets simultaneously, fed the information into the computer. All friendly ground vehicles, aerospace craft, and spacecraft were equipped with FIB's, Friendly Identification Beacons, that would be picked up by the radar and fed into the computer. The computer would assess all targets passed over to it by the radar, avoid the targets that had FIB markers, and in order of calculated threat, engage and destroy all targets until the gunner ordered a cease fire.

The navigator/bombardier was responsible for navigating the aerospace craft over great distances and for ground-support operations. For small targets, such as vehicles, equipment, and personnel; the navigator/bombardier could operate the belly pulse-laser cannon from his position in front of the cockpit while the gunner operated the dorsal turret. For larger targets, the Hellcat could be equipped with six variable-strength, computer-tracked, laser-guided bombs. Depending on the size and strength of the target, the navigator could quickly program the explosive power of the bombs together or individually and the point of detonation for surface, subsurface, or aerial detonations. With the variable-strength option, a bomb could be programmed to take out a portion of a single building up to an entire city block. Or the Hellcat could also be mounted with two class three torpedoes which were capable of engaging large ships at sea or in space.

With their powerful neutron accelerators, the small fighter-bombers were easily able to whip through the cosmic dust and stellar winds and out pace their mother ship. Zimmermann checked and double checked his onboard computer guidance system. Hera's orbital data gave them their bearing and they were rocketing at top speed towards her. But something wasn't right.

Hera belonged to a relatively small solar system containing six large, rocky planets, two of which were deemed inhabitable.

Edward O. Bast

But Hera was the best suited for immediate colonization because her atmosphere was breathable and already supported a myriad of life forms. The other planet, Athena, could be inhabited in a pinch, but her atmosphere would require extensive chemical enhancement to support life, and her closer proximity to the sun made her too hot and dry to exist without protective shelters. Presently, Athena supported no life, although the new inhabitants of Hera could one day occupy her in the distant future the same way that the Race had colonized Mars. The other planets were icy barren bergs of rock and dust with no activity except for Thor with its constant volcanic action.

Zimmermann and his Flight had entered Hera's system and, according to the computer, were headed right toward her, but the sensors onboard the fighter-bomber failed to pick her up. Zimmermann called down to his navigator/bombardier.

"Charlie, I'm still not picking anything up on my sensors; this can't be right."

"Beats the hell out of me, Hans. Do you want me to run diagnostics on it again?"

"Nah. Do you think something could be wrong with the computer?"

"I don't think so, Hans. Besides, the other birds are running on their own computers, too. All six computers can't be wrong. If we were veering off course, we would've heard from them."

"This shit stinks, Charlie. We're close enough we should have visual on her by now. I'm going to break radio silence and see if anyone else is picking her up." Hans Zimmermann switched off the Radio Listening Silence key on his communication system. "Black-bat one-two, this is Black-bat one-one, over."

After a brief pause, the familiar voice of Lieut. Sergey Kracsovichev, Zimmermann's wingman, came through the ear piece. "Good to hear from you, Hans. Listen, I'm not picking up Hera on my sensors; You got a fix on her?"

"No, that's why I called. Let me see if anyone else has got her. Break; Black-bat one-zero, this is one-one, does anybody read Hera?"

One by one, the other fighter-bombers of Flight Black-bat one-zero reported no evidence of the planet Hera.

"Okay, one-zero," Zimmermann sighed. "Stand by." Hans switched on the Intercom Only key. Charlie, what's our angle of approach on Hera's orbital plane?"

"Forty-seven degrees."

"All right. Let's drop down to zero degrees. That will expose our sensors to more of her orbit; maybe we can pick up something then."

"Roger, Hans. Inputting request into the computer now."

"Good. As soon as the computer calculates the flight adjustment, patch it over to the other birds."

"Right."

Zimmermann switched over to external comms. "Black-bat one-zero, this is one-one; I want to approach Hera on a different angle to see if we can pick her up. Charlie's inputting the flight path change now. As soon as it's up, he'll patch it over to you and we'll all execute on Formation Override."

Within a matter of seconds, the computer made the flight adjustment and Zimmermann's navigator/bombardier patched over the new flight data to the other five aerospace craft. Using the Formation Override, a control system in which the flight formation automatically follows the lead Hellcat without input or adjustment from the other pilots, Zimmermann dropped his Flight down to the new approach. As the formation of Hellcats smoothly and simultaneously changed its angle of attack on Hera, a voice rang out over Zimmermann's earphones.

"Holy shit. Do you see that?"

"No. What?" Zimmermann searched the darkness outside his canopy.

"This is one-four. Look where Hera's suppose to be; there are stars blinking on and off."

Zimmermann trained his eyes to around the point in space where the computer claimed Hera was. Their approach on Hera placed her sun ninety degrees to port, so the lost planet would be against a field of black besprinkled by a spattering of distant stars. The Flight's oblique path towards Hera caused the starry background to slide across their field of view. At the point where Hera should have been, stars momentarily blinked out and then back on again.

"Yeah, I see it," Zimmermann shouted over the net. Charlie aimed their sensors directly toward the phenomenon and narrowed the focus of their scan to provide maximum reading power to the black spot in space.

"I'm now picking up Hera's two moons but there ain't no planet. Nothing, Hans," Charlie gasped. "There ain't nothing there."

"I hear you, Charlie," Zimmermann said in a raised voice, his pulse quickening. "But we all see it. Take us there!"

"Hell, man. We're headed right for it."

As the formation of Hellcats zipped towards the ever growing black spot in space, Lieut. Hans Zimmermann fed the data back to the other flights and the Earth ship *Singapore*. He didn't want the tailing flights to run into the same confusion that they just had. Their speed was too great for Flight Black-bat one-zero to obtain confirmation of the other flights receiving the information; Zimmermann just had to trust that they copied.

When Hera was about the size of a basketball, Zimmermann switched to manual controls and slowed the flight down, lest they would collide with her. There were absolutely no signals bouncing off the black orb, and Charlie had difficulty judging her distance. Zimmermann aimed his flight to the outer edge of the planet to establish an orbit around Hera to see if he could determine what they were up against. As Flight Blackbat one-zero slowed into a close orbit around the blackened planet, they skirted around its edge to the sunny side. Still all instruments were reading nothing, like the planet didn't exist. It was completely black; like a hole in space

"It kind of looks like some sort of black cloud," Lieut. Kracsovichev came in over the earphones.

"Yeah, it's weird," Zimmermann responded softly, amazed at the sight below the Flight. He then addressed his gunner. "Ty, fire an oblique shot at the edge of the cloud. I want to see what happens."

"Aye, aye," Ensign Tyrone Washington acknowledged. A moment later a flash of dark red light bolted from Zimmermann's Hellcat, penetrated the black cloud and reappeared miles down range disappearing into space.

"Anybody note anything strange; any deflection or anything?" Zimmermann radioed to his Flight. No one noticed anything abnormal. "Okay, I tell you what," Lieut. Zimmermann announced over the comms as he switched off the Formation Override. "I'm going in. Sergey, I'm going to pop in and pop out. If I'm not out in five minutes, you got charge of the Flight."

"Roger," Lieut. Kracsovichev acknowledged.

"Sergey, take the Flight up to a higher and slower orbit. I don't want any chance of us colliding with each other if I have to come rocketing out of that shit. Also, send a SITREP (Situation Report) back to the other flights and the *Singapore*.

"Well," Zimmermann paused. "This is it. Wish me luck."

"You got it, Hans. See you in five mikes (minutes)."

"Right." Lieut. Zimmermann broke formation and started slowly down into the pitch black cloud below. Lieut.

Kracsovichev watched as the gray Hellcat containing his friends disappeared into the black abyss. When the aerospace craft was completely within the cloud, its radar signature disappeared off of Kracsovichev's screen. Sergey waited a moment and then took the remainder of the Flight to a higher, slower orbit.

The time ticked by; three minutes, then four, then five. No sign of Black-bat one-one came.

"What do you think, Kracsovichev? It's been five mikes," a familiar voice from one of the other Hellcats came in over the headset.

"Quiet on the net," Sergey said almost in a whisper as he stared at the radar screens for some sign of his comrades. Seven minutes went by, then nine, finally eleven and no sign of the Hellcat and it's daring crew.

"Come on, man," a second voice rang out. "It's been over eleven mikes; we can't float here all day, we got to do something."

"I said, 'quiet on the net,'" the young wingman replied with a louder voice.

"Sergey!?!"

"Shut up!" Lieut. Kracsovichev barked over the mike, his gaze never leaving the radar screen.

Two more minutes passed when suddenly a small blue blip appeared on Sergey's screen. He jerked his head up in time to see a black plume erupt from the clouds about fifty kilometers down range. A tiny silver-gray speck bolted straight up from the plume like a cork from a champagne bottle. Lieut. Kracsovichev knew the craft was friendly by the blue blip which indicated it was equipped with a FIB. He was about to try and make communication contact with the object when a loud and excited voice blasted over the earphones.

"Black-bat one-two, Black-bat one-two, this is one-one, over."

Sergey recognized the voice of his friend, sighed a breath of relief and answered the call.

"This is one-one," Lieut. Zimmermann continued. "I found them! I found them! I'm going to radio the ship; monitor the net. Charlie will pipe all computer data to you and the ship during my transmission. Do you copy?"

"Roger," Sergey replied.

Zimmermann continued. "Break, break. Earth ship *Singapore*, Earth ship *Singapore*, this is Black-bat one-one, this is Black-bat one-one; messages follows. I have made contact with the 14th; I say again, I have made contact with the 14th! They are heavily engaged with an unknown hostile force; I say again, they are heavily engaged with an unknown hostile force! They are taking casualties. Computer calculations of Hera's location and the location of the 14th on Hera are accurate. Incoming flights should fly off their computers and not by instruments. Hera is cloaked with an unknown cloud that masks all known radio and light waves. The cloud is approximately two k's (kilometers) thick. Once under the cloud cover, Hera is pitch black, but communications and instruments are viable for operations. Black-bat one-zero is going in hot, weapons-free, manual control; I say again, we are going in hot, weapons-free, manual control." Lieut. Zimmermann then addressed his flight.

"All right, guys. Did you copy that transmission?"

The Flight acknowledged as they closed in behind Black-bat one-one's Hellcat.

"I saw the battle. It was just on the horizon. Shit, the place was lit up and popping like New Year's Eve. I want to go down range and get on the other side of the 14th just in case the enemy force picked me up and is waiting for us."

"What are we facing, Hans?" Sergey came in over the comms.

"I'm not really sure. The 14th said they were heavily engaged with a superior hostile force and that they needed support ASAP."

"Superior force?" Sergey continued. "Are our weapons going to be effective?"

"Yeah. They said that their weapons were effective against the threat, but that there were just too many of them. Apparently, whoever they are, they also have forces on the ground. The 14th reported that one of their flanks was beginning to collapse. That wouldn't be from just an air threat." Zimmermann paused. "All right. Listen up boys and girls, this is what I want to do."

They would enter the black, eerie cloud cover single file maintaining a constant airspeed and angle of decent in order to keep from running into one another. Once under the cloud cover, they would execute a "fighting wedge" formation. This oblique formation offered the gunners the most optimum fields of fire with their pulse-laser cannons. With their first pass, Flight Black-bat one-zero would concentrate on eliminating as much of the air threat as possible. Thereafter, they would break into two groups. Black-bat one-one, one-three, and one-four would continue to concentrate on the air threat while the remainder of the Flight, under Lieut. Kracsovichev, would deal with the forces on the ground. They would fight until the Hellcats ran out of fuel and then take up defensive positions on the ground and continue to fight with their dorsal turret cannons. Hopefully, the next flight of Hellcats would reach them before they ran out of fuel and take over the fight.

Zimmermann aimed his Hellcat back into the black clouds. All went black and his instruments gave no readings from outside the ship. Even though the rest of his flight was right behind him, no evidence of their presence appeared on any of his monitors.

He knew the thickness of the clouds by measuring his speed, angle of descent, and time within the ominous black soup.

"Holy sheep shit," a voice whispered over the net as the Hellcats emerged from the bottom of the mysterious black clouds and the flashing fury of the 14th's desperate struggle for survival became fully in view. This was their first fight. To be sure, the Race had managed peace for several decades amongst themselves. There were but a few harden combat experience personnel left and they were generally stationed at the military training centers to train the newly enlisted personnel and newly commissioned officers. And although these last remaining combat vets were able to maintain their youth through the miracles of modern medicine, their experience was decades old.

"All right, guys," Lieut. Zimmermann's voice barked over the air. "Radar shows no blue FIB's in the air. Weapons free. If it flies, it dies. Let's do it!"

The Hellcats aligned themselves in the combat wedge formation and screamed towards the fiery chaos above their stricken comrades. It was pitch black below the clouds. Only the flashing lights of angry cannons and the burning wrecks of hapless casualties could be seen by the unaided eye. But with the Hellcats' instruments, the full battle could be brought into view on the heads-up displays.

As they entered the fray, Hans Zimmermann was the first to loose his cannons upon the enemy. His pulse-laser cannon ripped through the skin of a black, enemy, boomerang-shaped fighter sending a cascade of sparks and molten metal droplets into Hera's warm atmosphere. The surprised enemy pilot turned hard away from his attacker leaving a trail of splintered metal as the aircraft's ruptured side gave way to the tempest of air caused by the its high speed. Zimmermann watched as the damaged wing of the boomerang fighter disintegrated sending the doomed craft into an uncontrollable spin towards death on Hera's terra firma. 'Yes,' he thought. 'We can do this.'

Immediately the gunner found another target with the aid of the onboard computer. More red bolts of super-heated light energy burned through the air with the speed of lightning. At the one-o'clock high position a bright red and yellow flash lit the darkness as Ty Washington's pulse-laser cannons found another target. The blast from the exploding enemy fighter was so powerful; it shot bits of the disintegrating ship against Zimmermann's Hellcat. The cannon never skipped a beat as another hapless boomerang fighter turned on its side in a sharp turn in an effort to evade the Hellcats' fury only to be hit dead-center by Ty's red darts of death. The doomed fighter collapsed in two and then separated sending the two wide wings spinning freely down to the planet's surface.

Despite Lieut. Zimmermann's earlier descent below the clouds, Black-bat one-zero was able to catch the enemy totally unaware. Their first drive into the heart of the enemy, their cannons furiously barking out pulses of super-heated light energy every half second, dealt out a terrible blow as fourteen of the alien fighters plummeted to the surface of Hera and two others limped away from battle.

Because of the high number of enemy aircraft swarming around the sky like a perturbed swarm of angry bees, Zimmermann decided to continue the air battle longer before turning his wingman's attention to the ground battle. He figured each aircraft averaged about eight more minutes of fuel and he had to make every minute count. He gave the order to free attack, allowing the planes to break from the formation and assault enemy boogies on their own. Each Hellcat sought its own target and gave pursuit, their cannons spitting out red flashes of destruction.

The alien fighter craft had shaken off the initial shock of the surprise attack and countered with equal impetuosity. Their cannons brightened the darkness with yellow bolts of destructive energy, as the agile fighters maneuvered into attack positions. Unlike the Hellcats, whose cannons were mounted in quick, fully rotating turrets and able to engage a target from any angle of flight, the enemy boomerang fighters had to align their flight path with their target in order to get an effective shot. This was a decisive advantage for the outnumbered Hellcats. Their pilots could concentrate solely on flying, evading and outmaneuvering the enemy aircraft while the gunner and bombardier, with the aid of the onboard computer for aiming and tracking, could fight the aircraft. Unfortunately, each of the Hellcat's cockpits' fuel warning lights were blinking and buzzing, alerting the crews that time was running out.

As Lieut. Zimmermann defiantly maneuvered Black-bat one-one through the maelstrom of darting aircraft and yellow rays of destruction, he sized up the situation. Each Hellcat carried ten minutes of reserve fuel which was only to be used in time of war. This classified for that, he thought. But the purpose of the fuel was to break contact from the enemy and find a safe place to land so the precious fighter and her crew could live to fight another day. He wanted to stay on station until the next Flight arrived, at least. Zimmermann had to make a decision, a decision that could decide the fate of his entire flight of six fighter craft and eighteen men and women. He ordered the pilots to stay and fight.

By now the black sky was somewhat lightened by cannon and fire light reflecting off the smoke emitted from burning and exploding aircraft. The aliens did not have a strategy for fighting the versatile Hellcats; not this time. Zimmermann's Black-bat one-zero was winning the day. Despite the outnumbered Hellcats, their crews proved quite worthy. The air buzzed and hummed with the silent boomerang craft slicing through it.

The Hellcats' guns gave a terrible sound, not loud, but strangely muffled. The air reek of an ionized plasma from the discharging of the pulse-laser cannons. It was saturated with an acidic sweet odor of electricity and steel. Suddenly...

"One-one, this is one-four. I'm hit; I'm hit."

Zimmermann jumped at the sudden blast over the radio. He twisted and turned in the cockpit, jerking his head around to try and spot his stricken comrade. "One-four, where are you? Where are you?

"I'm hit; I can't hold her, I'm losing her."

"Eject, dammit, eject," Zimmermann continued to scan the skies, but he could not find his friends.

"I gotta wait. I think Barbara's still in the gun turret. I've lost comms. I wanna be sure she's in the capsule."

Ensign Barbara Brochmann was the gunner of Black-bat one-four. A capable officer, and a solid, good woman; she was highly regarded by all in Zimmermann's Flight, albeit often teased in good humor by the men who respected her most.

"You gotta punch out, Dennis," Zimmermann screamed in the mike at one-four's pilot. "Where's Sandy?" Dennis had not mentioned the fate of his navigator/bombardier.

"He's gone," the frantic pilot began to cry. "We got hit broadside, fore and aft of the cockpit. My God, Hans. I think I've lost my crew."

"Punch out, Dennis. Damn you, eject, eject," Zimmermann pleaded angrily into the mike. Suddenly, at Hans Zimmermann's three o'clock, a bright flash brightened the dark sky and the radio went momentarily dead.

Lieut. Zimmermann stared mouth agape as the fiery orange ball hurled itself to Hera's earth, but his attention was quickly drawn back to the radio as another frantic voice shattered the silence of the net.

"This is one-three; I'm going down. I'm hit!"

"One-three, this is one-one; come in."

"We're breaking up, Hans. We're all in the capsule; we're punching out."

"Go on, get out of there, Martin," Zimmermann yelled. Then another voice rang over the headsets.

"This is one-six. We've just taken a hit in the nose. The capsule is damaged; it's lost its structural integrity. I'm going to try to put her down somewhere."

Lieut. Zimmermann couldn't believe his ears. His Flight was breaking apart, their luck had run out. Hans looked out the front of his canopy just in time to see a boomerang fighter swoop around and come straight at the Hellcat's nose, its cannons blazing. 'This is it,' he thought. 'It's over.'

Suddenly, the enemy ship erupted into a large ball of molten steel and fire as six Hellcats screeched across Black-bat one-one's flight path, their guns popping incessantly.

"Black-bat one-one, this is Black-bat two-one. Do you read me, Hans?" Lieut. Zimmermann recognized the voice of his fellow flight leader, Lieutenant Michael Boone on the headset.

"Mike, is that you?" Zimmermann said practically holding his breath.

"Yeah. Sorry we're late old buddy, but we came through that black cloud on the wrong side of the planet."

Zimmermann sighed in relief. "Mike, I gotta get my Flight out of here. I'm down three birds and we are out of fuel."

"I hear that, Hans," Lieut. Boone replied. "Get out of here, man. We got it. Black-bat three-zero should be here shortly, as well."

"Good luck, Mike." Zimmermann then radioed the remainder of his Flight to land at the 14th Terrestrial Division airstrip.

Through the gray smoke-filled sky, the three last aircraft of Black-bat one-zero broke contact with the enemy and headed for the unlit airstrip near the center of the beleaguered 14th's defensive positions. With the battle still raging overhead and along the perimeters of the 14th's shaky hold on the ground, the three Hellcats landed gently on the tarmac. Once on the ground, Lieut. Zimmermann looked up at the show far above their heads as Lieut. Mike Boone and his boys and girls battled it out with the alien invaders. Hans was shortly joined by his other two crews. Lieut. Yoshiko Matsuo, commander of Black-bat one-five, came up and stood directly in front of her flight leader.

"I think we lost Barbara, Yoshiko," Zimmermann said weakly. "I'm sorry. I know how close you two were."

"I know," Lieut. Matsuo said softly. She then reached up and wrapped her arms around Hans' neck and kissed him gently on the cheek. Yoshiko leaned back and looked Hans dead in the eyes. "Now get us back up there in the fight," the firmness that everyone was accustomed was back in Matsuo's throat. "I want to kick some more alien ass."

Zimmermann looked over at his wingman Lieut. Sergey Kracsovichev. "You ain't got us no fuel yet, Sir?" Sergey said with a half smile curled across his lips.

Zimmermann turned to an Army major who had come running out to meet the naval flight crews when they touched down. "Sir, we need some fuel."

The major turned to one of his men. "Sergeant Lacey, get some fuel rods over here, quick."

CHAPTER THREE

When Lieut. Zimmerman's initial message about the attack on Hera had reached the *Singapore*, Adm. Rodriguez deployed every fighter craft, save one flight to protect the carrier and her escorts, to the embattled planet. Within hours, the skies over Hera were swarming with Hellcats that were shooting anything that moved on the ground or in the air that didn't register a blue dot on the FIB's. The aliens, soon outnumbered and outgunned, turned and took what remained of their attack force and withdrew behind the shield of the same mysterious black cloud that had cloaked their advance and covered the planet. The stars once again appeared over Hera as the thick, abstruse, pall-like mist released its choking grip and soared back in the direction it had come. Permission to pursue the enemy masked within the cloud was denied the battle-eager Hellcat pilots. Perhaps this was enough to ward off further attacks, perhaps another enemy force, an even larger force, was en route. In any event, 5th Frontier Fleet Space Command did not wish the loss of any more aircraft or crew until all the data could be analyzed and the Fleet had a better idea of what it was it was up against.

With the black cloud gone, communications were once again opened between the 14th Terrestrial Division and III Intergalactic Corps. No contact with the Earth ship *Ottawa*, set in longitudinal orbit around the planet before the attack, had been re-established and the 14th feared the worse. Hellcats had been sent out to search the planet, but no sign of the missing space ship had yet to be found.

The battle had lasted thirty some odd hours and taken a tremendous toll on the unexpecting division. The 14th Terrestrial Division was basically an engineering and research division. Although not unarmed, it was not a combat unit and therefore ill-equipped to take on such a large attack force that was sent against her. The Hellcats, with their superior versatility and firepower, had definitely won the day. With the battle over, the 14th went about attending the wounded, preparing the dead for burial, assessing damages to the operation, and most importantly, preparing for the next attack.

The research units were especially busy, but not with research on Hera herself. The research units were fully occupied with learning about the aliens who had attacked them. Destroyed boomerang fighter craft littered the ground for more than 2,500 square kilometers, burnt out enemy vehicles were scattered around the entire perimeter, and more excitingly, the remains of the aliens who had occupied them.

The enemy had not had time nor was in the position to extract their dead or dying. This gave the 14th concern that there might still be aliens alive and combat capable stranded on Hera. Combat patrols had been dispatched to seek out and capture, kill if necessary, any surviving aliens that could be found. Reconnaissance patrols, both aerial and on the ground, were sent out to ensure that the aliens had not established any kind of bases on the planet. Hera also had two moons, Ares and Hebe. These had not been initially seen by Flight, Black-bat one-zero, until it changed the angle of its approach because of their positioning at that time on the opposite side of the planet. Although not life-supporting, they were both massive and could easily conceal large contingents of fighting forces and equipment. These too, would have to be checked. The situation on Hera was in no way secure, and the Race had to maintain a steady vigilance.

Earth ship *Singapore* with her two escorts, the *Hiroshima* and the *Boston*, were the first to arrive in orbit around Hera. The remaining Hellcats returned to their carrier for maintenance to prepare them for another possible battle. A total of five Hellcats had been lost and several were damaged including Black-bat one-six that got the nose hit and had to seek refuge on the ground, but whose crew was saved to fight another day.

Others were not so lucky. Besides the five aircrews lost from the *Singapore*, the 14th suffered dozens of casualties especially in the light combat brigades. They would not be able to stave off another attack. Reinforcements were needed. Unfortunately, III Intergalactic Corps was not combat heavy so very little in reinforcements was readily available. It would take years to get anything from earth so reinforcements would have to be enlisted and trained from the civilian immigrants packed inside the cargo ships en route for Hera. But even then the first transport ship was not to arrive for another forty-five days and the rest would follow piecemeal for the next year and a half.

Immediate help would have to come from the 1st Marine Brigade doled out in the Fleet's escort ships. The brigade headquarters and the 1st Battalion were on the Earth ship *Hiroshima*; the 2nd Battalion was on the *Boston*. These two battalions would shoulder most of the weight of security until the 3rd Battalion on the *Saõ Paulo* and the 4th Armored Battalion on the *Milan* arrived in three days time.

Aboard the *Hiroshima*, the 1st Marine Battalion was boarding the landing shuttles that would ferry them down to a secure area within the perimeter of the 14th Terrestrial Division. From there it would move out to extend the Race's fragile hold on Hera, check for possible enemy, and prepare the way for the incoming flood of warriors and immigrants.

Lieutenant Colonel Glenda Carter, Commander of the 1st Battalion, called her company commanders together one last time before they would meet again on Hera soil. Once her company commanders had gathered, Lt Col. Carter removed her helmet and looked at each one in turn: Headquarters Company Commander, Captain Mary Hartmann; Alpha Company Commander, Captain Brian Montgomery; Bravo Company

Commander, Captain Richard Braun; and Charlie Company Commander, Captain Nina Errington.

"This is it, guys," Lt Col. Carter said utterly deadpan. "Remember, when we hit the ground link up with your liaison from the 14th; they'll be waiting for you. They will guide you through their unit lines and release you once you're past their positions. Keep in contact with each other," Carter continued. "And when we get to our defensive objectives start digging in. Be sure you're in contact with each other on the flanks; no gaps. We will meet again at my CP at 1800 Mean Hera Time for a status check. Questions?" Everyone signified none. "Good,' she concluded. Get back to your units, and we'll see you on the ground."

Nina turned to Cpt. Hartmann. "How's the Science Officer holding out, Mary?"

Mary Hartmann smiled. "He's holding out fine, a little nervous perhaps, but he's doing just fine."

"When's he going in?"

"With the first wave, with the S-3 (Operations)." Mary paused; she could sense her friend's anxiety. "Come on, Nina. Go pop in and check on him before you go back to your company."

Nina smiled sheepishly and followed Cpt. Hartmann through the hive of busy naval and marine personnel loading supplies and boarding the landing crafts for debarkation. When they arrived at the Battalion Staff's loading point, she found Ben supervising the loading of his equipment aboard one of the landing craft.

"All set to go, Captain Errington?" Nina said compassionately.

Ben turned to see Nina, decked out in her combat gear. He smiled weakly. "Some honeymoon cruise, huh?" he chuckled.

"I'd have thought you'd be excited about seeing intelligent aliens," Nina joked in an effort to lighten his anxiety.

"Well, yeah," he smirked. "But I'd prefer them not shooting at me."

Nina walked up to her husband and gave him a light peck on the cheek. "I'll see you on the ground," she smiled and turned back through the throng of sailors and marines preparing to shuttle to Hera terra firma.

The barges were quickly and systematically loaded with equipment, supplies, and the marines that would use them. From the belly of the *Hiroshima*, ten barges constituting half of Lt. Col. Carter's battalion emerged like larva from an insect's egg pod. Since no enemy had really been planned, the landing barges were pretty much defenseless except for two light pulse lasers each. As soon as the barges cleared the *Hiroshima*, they were immediately swarmed by several Hellcats that would escort them safely to Hera's surface.

Cpt. Ben Errington gripped firmly the arm rest of the seat in which he was securely belted as the barge slipped effortlessly into the black void surrounding Hera. These seats were not as well cushioned as the ones he'd grown accustomed on *Enos nine-two*. Although he did not feel as safe and comfortable as he had on *Enos nine-two*, he was now in a position of responsibility with subordinates under him and therefore could not allow himself the luxury of feeling scared much less showing it in front of his people.

As soon as they left the gravity field of Earth ship *Hiroshima*, small, overlooked items began to float around inside the troop/cargo bay of the barge. As much time as Ben was spending in space, little of it was in a weightless setting. Long term weightlessness was neither beneficial to the human body nor conducive to work. He was momentarily drawn away from the urgent mission they were partaking and was amused at the small bolts, pins, and other miscellaneous objects floating and bumping into each other in the troop/cargo bay. But no sooner had the unsecured objects began to float around in the bay than they began to settle back down to the floor and finally landing with thuds as the barge entered into Hera's atmosphere and gravity.

From the portal on the opposite side of the bay, Ben could see the bright glow outside as the barge dove into ever increasing atmospheric pressure. The ride became rough as the barge twisted and rolled in the thickening atmosphere of their new planet, bucking and jerking as it made its way to a landing spot near the front lines of the 14th Terrestrial Division. Shortly the bright glow outside of the ship disappeared and Dr. Errington could see the dark blue sky fading the stars as it brightened. Occasionally he'd glimpse one of the escorting Hellcats in the distance as they followed the barges down. Graceful birds, the Hellcats, but with deadly talons that had already proven themselves in combat. Ben felt comforted by their presence. Back in his time, Dr. Errington was considered somewhat a pacifist. But now he wanted all the firepower around him the fleet could muster. Now he understood that a good defense lay in offensive capabilities.

From the belly of the barge he could hear the landing doors opening and the high whine of the landing gear screws lowering the gear as they made their approach on the landing sites. With a slight clunk, the landing gear was locked into place. Despite the protective skin of the barge, Ben could distinctively hear the air rush and drag against the landing struts. Then with a slight jolt, the ship settled on Hera's soil. No one spoke as the cargo doors opened and the bright sunlight evaded the subtle hues of the cargo bay. Blinding at first, the light was as intrusive as the scent of wildflowers that rushed in to overtake the nondescript air of the spaceship. Ben drew in a deep nose's worth of the poignant odor that seemed a cross between cinnamon and anise.

Suddenly the cargo bay came to life as sergeants began barking orders for disembarking and unloading the landing barge. Time was of the greatest importance now as the barges had to return to the Earth ship *Hiroshima* to ferry down the other half of the battalion. Ben grabbed his personal gear and headed toward the piercing bright light outside the ship. His eyes quickly adjusted and he found his section sergeant, Gunnery Sergeant William Sanderson, herding his small section together to start unloading their equipment and supplies. Once the barge was unloaded, their equipment was reloaded onto all-terrain vehicles or CMPVs (Combat Multi-purpose Vehicles, pronounced 'comp-vee'). These eight-wheeled cargo carriers were joined in three places allowing each pair of wheels to support its own section which provided the vehicle excellent terrain negotiation capabilities as it snaked its way along practically any uneven surface.

After assuring that his section, the Battalion Scientific Research Section, was ready to proceed to their deployment location, Cpt. Errington joined his team with the rest of the Operations Section.

The Operations Officer, Major Brent Southerland, huffed his way into the mix. This was his day to shine. He was due to be reviewed for promotion, and the idea of being a primary staff officer for a Marine Combat Battalion during actual hostile operations was his ticket for his two silver diamonds, the insignia of a lieutenant colonel. Maj. Southerland strutted about like a peacock in heat, but with little to do as the staff's noncommissioned officers already had everything under control.

The marine line companies deployed out to about three kilometers from the 14th's outer positions. With combat units securing the perimeter, the 14th Terrestrial Division could take a breath and begin to lick its wounds. The 1st Marine Battalion set its headquarters up on a grassy knoll concealed by tall tree-like plants that stood defiantly everywhere. Pungent scents of exotic flowers permeated the warm afternoon air as the marines worked feverously to ready their positions and headquarters before nightfall. Patrols had been sent out as soon as the perimeter lines were established. Drones buzzed over the thick treetops searching out any signs of alien life. Captain Errington's science section started immediately to test the vegetation and any other small life it could find for toxin levels that might affect the marines. Linked in to the data base established by the 14th, a fair amount of information had already been compiled.

In Charlie Company Cpt. Nina Errington was making the last minute checks on her perimeter. Her platoon leaders briefed her on each of their lines of responsibility in turn. Her portion of the perimeter put the left half of her company in a thick forested area. It was defendable but much of the underbrush had to be cut away to provide adequate fields of fire for her Marines. The other half overlooked a large meadow with a dry stream bed snaking a broad path across its breadth. She checked her lines with solid military expertise, but all the while she kept an eye on her watch. She did not want to be late for the 1800 hour battalion commander's meeting and another chance to see her husband.

Hera had about a twenty-one and a half hour day. C.O.P.E. had established its base near the equator to provide the new civilization a moderate climate during the initial phases of getting established. Their location also meant that the daylight hours and nighttime hours were relative equal. At this time of the year, the forces could rely on about ten hours of daylight each day. The 1800 hour meeting was therefore at night and all positions must be ready before the company commanders could leave their units and meet at the battalion headquarters.

Nina watched as the evening sun ignited Hera's sky in brilliant shades of red and blue. One of her moons was already high in the late afternoon sky as the second began to peak out from under the veil of treetops that crested the horizon. She knew that one of them was named Ares and the other Hebe, but she wasn't sure which one was which. Nina reached into her right pants leg pocket and pulled out a food bar. Slowly, almost methodically, she unwrapped the chocolate-flavored, nutrient-packed field ration while staring off into the distance. As Cpt. Errington slowly began to nibble on her evening fare, she lowered her eyes from the sky and out into the darkening trees below the horizon. Unconsciously she rolled each morsel around in her mouth as she weighed her options and her emotions in her mind. She would have to tell Ben sooner or later. Worse yet, she would have to tell Lt Col. Carter. What would this mean to her command; her career? She was right where she wanted to be and this war; this war. She and her comrades have spent their careers preparing for just such a possibility, and now that it's here…

Nina thought about Maj. Southerland, the Operations Officer. He was definitely in his element. He saw the war as a gateway to enhancing his own career. Indeed, many of the officers, and probably the non-commissioned officers as well, viewed this as an opportunity to excel, but for Nina Errington, the timing was way off. Swallowing the morsel she looked down at her half eaten food bar. Yes, she must tell Ben, the sooner the better.

The company commanders shuffled into the Tactical Operations Center, the TOC, and greeted each other with smiles and chuckles. From the small talk, one would never surmise that there was a war on. They drifted over to the map and informally briefed Maj. Southerland about their positions, potential problems, and the readiness of their units. Using their hands as pointers, each commander indicated his positions on the map to the Operations Officer, who nodded his approval.

The TOC was a mobile command center and therefore pretty lean. It consisted of light, telescoping tubing for a frame and a canvas-like covering that protected the people inside from weather, chemical or biological agents, radiation, small arms fire, and light shrapnel. The outside of the layer of the covering consisted of Chameleon Coat, a fibrous translucent fabric that picked up the light reflected from where it touched a hard surface, like the ground or a tree and assimilated those colors helping it to blend in with its environs. So if it were touching snow, it would look white; the desert would turn it the color of the sand it were touching, and so on.

The inside was an off-white so people could see better with limited light. The walls also functioned as computer screen where maps could be displayed as well as presentation slides or any other image that could be put into a computer. The covering also protected it's marines from heat of day or cold weather down to a -50 c. Finally it had an inner layer of woven spider's thread. Tougher than steel, this light, flexible material could easily stop small projectiles such as shrapnel.

Cpt. Ben Errington was at his work station in the TOC making final preparations for his portion of the briefing. He would come after the Intelligence Officer's briefing on the known enemy situation and the weather. Ben would inform the commanders on known toxic plants or vectors with which their marines might come in contact. Nina wanted desperately to tell Ben her news, but she saw that he was much too busy to bother at this moment. It would have to wait.

Lt Col. Glenda Carter entered the TOC and someone called 'At ease!' to bring the company commanders' and staff's attention to the Battalion Commander. She immediately waded into the group of officers huddled around the map and briefly studied the lines depicting the battalion's perimeter. Glenda then turned and nodded at her XO.

"Ladies and gentlemen," Maj. Hajime Koyama announced to everyone in the TOC. "Please take your seats so we can get this briefing started." The XO waited until everyone was seated and then turned to the Commander. "Ma'am, everyone is present. We'll start tonight with an update on the enemy situation." Koyama nodded to the Intel Officer and took his seat.

Cpt. Nina Errington listened to each of the briefers in turn. She was so proud of Ben when he got up and addressed the commanders and staff on the toxic plants and vectors known on Hera. He had come a long way from the shy, twenty-first century paleontologist she had plucked out of the Montana Big Open four years ago.

Finally, each company commander briefed his current status to the battalion commander and staff. Briefings were old hat for Nina, as they were for most of the officers. But this situation was not an exercise and Lt Col. Carter leaned forward in her chair as she listened to her company commanders. She had to be prepared. She couldn't allow her battalion to be the weak link in the perimeter.

The enemy situation was unsure. To the Races' knowledge, they had kicked the aliens off Hera and back from whence they came. But two questions remained unanswered for the III Intergalactic Corps of the 5th Frontier Fleet: were there any stragglers left behind on Hera when the aliens withdrew and would the aliens return?

After the last briefer, Lt Col. Carter stood up and gave her theory and priorities. She was always serious, but tonight there was a bit of uncertain urgency in her words. "...to be sure," she concluded. "The Race has never encountered such an enemy and we were taken totally off guard when we found out what we're fighting. Or perhaps I should say 'whom.' And now, thanks to the efforts of the 14th Terrestrial Division, I present you the enemy." She turned to Ben, "Doctor Errington." Glenda Carter always referred to Ben as 'doctor' when she wanted to emphasis to her officers his professional background, giving credence to what he said.

Ben nodded and he turned to his section sergeant, "Gunnery Sergeant Sanderson." As Sanderson and a couple marines momentarily left the TOC, Ben Errington went back up to the front of the small briefing area. "As we are all aware the 14th had close and direct contact with the aliens a few nights ago. Casualties were taken on both sides. Thanks to our brave men and women in the death-dealing Hellcats, the aliens had to beat a hasty retreat to wherever. Doing so, they left behind many of their dead." Ben paused for a moment and glanced expectantly at the TOC flap where his subordinates had disappeared.

"Due to the lethality of our weapons systems," Ben continued as he brought his attention back to his audience. "Most of the dead aliens have been rendered to mere body parts strewn over the Hera landscape. However," he sighed. "A few of the aliens, those hit primarily indirectly through shrapnel, remained intact enough that it didn't take a paleontologist to put them back together." Nina smiled at the insinuation. "This afternoon the 14th sent us a viable specimen."

Gunnery Sergeant Sanderson and his marines reentered the TOC with a gurney. On the gurney was unmistakably a body covered with a white sheet. As they stood the gurney on end to better facilitate viewing, the company commanders leaned forward on their chairs. The figure beneath the sheet had a familiar outline, a head, a torso, and two legs. Ben reached up and grabbed the part of the sheet that was tucked in beneath the head. He tugged the sheet loose and let it fall to the floor of the TOC. "Ladies and gentlemen, to quote a line, 'we have discovered the enemy and he is us.'"

Mouths dropped open as the commanders and members of the staff that had yet seen the alien glanced upon it for the first time. Before them, strapped to the gurney, was the nude body of a young woman; perfect in almost every detail, except for the large gaping wound in her abdomen that was the apparent cause of her demise. The room was dead quite as everyone searched her features; her short brown hair, the soft features of her oval face, her square shoulders, her two ripe breasts, and her long slender legs. Then suddenly everyone spoke at once.

"That's an alien?" "You sure it ain't one of ours?" "It's a woman! We're fighting women?" "My God!" "This can't be right." "Are you sure?" "Is it human?"

Dr. Errington raised his hand to get his fellow officers' attention. "She's only around 99% human. The other fraction of one percent, we're not sure, but we're pretty sure it didn't come from planet earth."

"Where did it come from?" someone blurted.

"We're not sure," Ben shrugged.

Bravo Company commander, Cpt. Braun, raised his hand, "Are the males the same?"

"There are no males," Cpt. Ben Errington replied as eyebrows rose. "All specimens found to date have been female. Indications are we are fighting an army of women."

Cpt. Hartmann raised her hand, "Did they originate from earth?"

Ben took in a deep breath. "They are too human not to have had. Genetic testing of several specimens indicates that the foreign genetic material was introduced many generations ago."

"How many generations?"

"Don't know for sure. But it appears to be for several centuries. Back in the latter half of the twentieth century there were many reports of alien abductions. Now we know that except for yours truly," Ben smirked. "C.O.P.E. did not remove anyone from earth. Mars doesn't have the technology as do any of the other planets we colonized. Another intelligent organism had to have done it."

"Why just females?"

"Without a base population to proliferate the species, artificial insemination or a type of cloning had to be used. Females have the uterus for fetal development, men don't. If you clone a woman, you're going to get a woman and she can easily give birth to her own cloned offspring. If you're going to pick a sex to build a working population, females are the best choice."

"Why then the introduction of foreign genetic material?"

"Perhaps an attempt to avoid genetic weakening, or to remove an undesired characteristic, or even introduce a desired genetic trait," Dr. Errington shrugged. "It apparently doesn't have anything to do with outward appearances; it would be difficult to tell without a living specimen."

"Could we mate with them?" Every turned, tongue in cheek, and stared at Cpt. Montgomery, the battalion's swinger among the officers.

"Hey. I'm just curious scientifically, of course," he defended.

"Yes, we probably could," Ben smiled. "How much of the alien genetic trait would be passed on to the offspring is questionable, as is the possibility of any harmful effects it might have on the child.

"We also have no idea of the mental state of these creatures. The alien genetic material introduced into the system could have changed them physiologically. We would need to test."

"So these aren't superwomen?" Lt Col. Carter asked in an effort to ensure her officers. "We are really only fighting different technology, am I correct, Doctor?"

"Yes, Ma'am. All initial research indicates that these women are, physically at least, no different than any woman in this TOC."

"Finally, this is the uniform she was wearing." Ben held up a blue and silver two-piece. "Obviously not the uniform of a field soldier," he continued. "We believe she was an officer. The 14th is piecing together a field uniform so to assist you in alien identification, but until then the general rule of thumb is as the Intel Officer said, if it doesn't look like us, it isn't."

"Okay, thank you, Dr Errington. Any further questions?" Lt Col. Carter asked turning to her officers. No one responded. "Okay then. Keep your pickets alert tonight. Let's get back to work." As she stood up from her chair, everyone in the TOC came to the position of attention. She turned to Ben and Nina. "I would like to see you two in my office," she said poker-faced, turned and exited the TOC.

CHAPTER FOUR

Captains Ben and Nina Errington followed the C.O. at a quick step to her office. Ben looked at Nina and mouthed 'What?' but she could only look at him with a weak smile and shrug her shoulders. She had a good idea 'what,' but she couldn't tell him on the run; not like this.

They followed Lt Col. Carter into her office where she marched behind her desk, spun on her toes to face them, and planted both fists, knuckles down, firmly on her desk.

"Well," she started as she glared at them both. "I had a very interesting conversation with the PA (Physician's Assistant) today." Glenda paused and took in a deep breath before her next shot. "I don't know whether to congratulate you or to chew your asses out good."

Nina lowered her head as though in shame. Not because of anything she had done, but because of what she had not done. Ben, having been taken totally off guard, just stood there mouth agape like he had just been shot in the gut. Glenda measured their responses and readdressed Ben.

"Ben, you look like you don't know what I'm talking about." He slowly shook his head in complete bewilderment. "For the love of Mary, Nina! Haven't you even told him?"

"No, Ma'am," Nina confessed. "I found out in the midst of all this happening, and…well, there just hasn't been a good moment."

Glenda gestured her head towards Ben. "Well? Or shall I tell him?"

Nina shook her lowered head, still ashamed that it had to come out this way. "Ben, I'm sorry I didn't tell you sooner, but I found out a couple of days ago that I'm; we're, going to have a baby."

Ben was speechless. He couldn't take his eyes off of Nina, but he couldn't find the words he wanted to say either.

Lt Col. Carter continued. "What am I suppose to do now, Nina? I can't have a pregnant woman in command of a line company; especially during time of war." She lowered her head and shook it slowly from side to side. "I'm going to have to transfer you."

"No," Nina begged.

"Nina, we're at war. I need a commander in top physical condition; it's only fair to the company." Glenda paused for a moment. "Think of the baby. I know you don't want to endanger it."

"Ma'am, please, don't transfer me. I understand I'll lose the command, but let me stay with the battalion. Please."

"Nina, I don't think it wise that I keep a pregnant woman on the front line during time of war. We must consider the baby."

"Ma'am, please. I can work in the headquarters; I'll do anything. I just don't want to be separated from Ben."

"Nina, even if I kept you, it could only be until your third trimester." Glenda made an outward gesture with her arms spread wide, "Surely you don't want the baby born here."

Nina lowered her head as she contemplated the hopelessness of her situation. This was exactly what she had feared. This was the exact reason she had been reluctant to tell anyone what should have been joyful news.

The three stood in silence until Glenda finally spoke. "Ah, shit. Okay, Nina. I'll do what I can to keep you two together."

She glanced over at Ben standing quietly, staring into space with a grin from ear to ear. "What the hell are you smiling at?"

Ben looked at her with his big broad smile and proclaimed, "I'm going to be a daddy." Nina hiccupped a laugh, her head still lowered.

Even Glenda couldn't suppress a smile. "Get out of here; both of you," she said shaking her head.

The next day saw a morning sun set against a cloudless blue sky. Off in the distance some animal chirped in the dry, still air. Form following function, most of the animals the Race had encountered on Hera were of the four legged variety. Some were large, like the herd discovered migrating across a plain to the north. Measuring over three meters at the shoulder, these long-neck, thick-tail, hairless, grey creatures with small heads were grazers and of no threat to the Race. Some were small, lizard-like motley creatures and colorful green and grey spotted rodent-size hoppers that bounced along the ground like kangaroo rats, but herded like lemmings on migration to the sea. There were medium-sized grazers with long, thick tails, thick armor-like brown skin, and half meter long black horns above each brown eye. These egg layers were being considered for domestication for food for the Race.

They had also discovered at least one predator; a large lion-size creature with a long, thick tail and fangs like a saber-toothed tiger. This ferocious meat eater had strong long hind legs and was often seen standing bipedally. Its front legs were shorter so its hips were taller than its shoulders when it stood on all fours. At the end of each muscular forearm was a clawed four-fingered hand. Three of the fingers pointed forward while the last digit, situated at the wrist, pointed to the rear. It could, however, swing this fourth digit forward like an opposable thumb allowing the creature to grasp. One had been dispatched, and the exploratory dissection revealed a large, developed brain. It was, perhaps, the most intelligent creature on Hera.

There were also fliers. These feathered creatures still sported long slender tails. Some were brightly colored suggesting that their eyes were adapted to seeing colors. Some sported beaks but many had lizard-like heads with small rows of sharp teeth. They reminded Ben Errington of prehistoric birds that once flew earth's infant skies.

Insect-type vectors were a problem on Hera. Just as on earth, there were crawling ones, flying ones, and even swimming ones. There was even one stinging type, called mosquitoes for lack of a better term, which would light on its host and suck blood for its protein. It left a painful red sore that would normally inflame and fester for one or two days. Fortunately, Hera also produced a fruit that these flying vampires detested. Similar to the lemon, this acetic fruit was encased in a thick, spongy, moist rind like an orange that housed a chemical toxic to Hera's mosquito. Squeeze or twist the rind and it sprayed this chemical into the air. Applying it to skin or clothing kept these worrisome pests at bay.

Plant life was also abundant on Hera. Many of the grains, fruit, nuts, tubers, and leafy plants were proving edible, nutritious, and could be easily cultivated. There was in particular an abundant fruit, high in protein and some essential vitamins, that tasted a lot like boiled peanuts. Easily picked and shelled, it was a favorite among the marines and soldiers of the units presently occupying and settling Hera.

This planet offered its new inhabitants much: good fertile land, oceans and rivers teaming with aquatic life, abundant food supplies, and an agreeable climate. The only fly in the ointment was a race of intelligent aliens determined to keep the Race off the planet. And the fact was that these aliens, the ones that the 14th fought at least, were for the most part, human.

Ben was back in his lab this fine morning examining and testing various plant tissues. Even though the Race was hunkering down for another possible attack, men and women in Cpt. Errington's field were moving ahead with preparations for the soon to be arriving immigrants. The brass of the 5th Frontier Fleet felt there was no recourse but to continue full steam towards Hera as planned and Hera had to be ready for them.

While he worked he couldn't help but to think of his new baby growing inside of Nina's womb. He wondered if it would be the first Heran born on this planet. Probably not, he reluctantly conceded. Surely there were other pregnant women aboard the ships to be arriving soon that were further along than Nina was. Nonetheless, his child would be one of the first, one of the first generations of true Herans, and that made Ben proud. A smile found its way back onto his lips.

But what kind of future would his baby face here? Cpt. Errington glanced over at the alien corpse lying half frozen in the specimen preserving capsule; a pretty young woman. She seemed to be in her early twenties or even late teens. Of course with the age reducing formulas floating around so much these days, who could tell how old anyone really was. And space travel made time all but pointless. He was from the twentieth century and Nina, the thirty-second, but he was only a few years older than she. They had spent only two of their years traveling to Hera due to the fleet's tremendous speed, but everyone they knew back on earth would be long dead by now. In order to get back to the time they left earth, they would have to travel through a wormhole to some time in the distant past and then fly forward in time to some point in earth time just after they had left earth. And in fact, that was the plan for much of the C.O.P.E. military personnel; to return to the thirty-second century earth, at least for those who would survive this war.

Ben looked back down at the frozen naked body of the young alien. He wondered how far she had traveled, and would she be missed? Did she have a family or at least a mother, or were these poor human-like creatures raised and treated like so many ants? He wondered what her planet must be like. Had they planned to inhabit Hera first to find us already here and then decided to try and remove us by force? Or were we trespassing on some world to which her race laid claim? Would they come back to get her?

Cpt. Nina Errington had briefed her platoon leaders upon returning to the company from the TOC the night before. Each was to send out squad size patrols to comb the area to their direct front for any signs of enemy presence. Overhead drones constantly buzzed back and forth in search of any possible aliens left behind, so her marines had to ensure that their FIB's were working. The patrols had deployed shortly after breakfast and she waited anxiously in the company CP (command post) for any word from them.

The sophisticated CP had several computer screens. One was a map of the area in which each patrol member could be located and traced by the little blue dots set off by their FIB's, picked up by overhead satellite, and patched down to the company's computer system which then posted the locations on the CP map in real time.

Three other screens were split into ten smaller screens each and the smaller screens projected the images patched in by small cameras mounted in each patrol member's helmet. Each of the larger screens were monitored by a marine in the CP thereby receiving real time information on exactly what the patrol members were seeing. Since the marines on the ground were constantly turning their heads from one side to the other, the images often flew by in blurred shades of green, brown, and blue. Nina had tried to watch for a little while, but the constant motion made her nauseous, an effect she assumed was caused by her pregnancy.

Each patrol member also had a mike set mounted in his helmet so that he could talk easily to the other members of his patrol, even at some distance through background noise. He could also communicate directly with his platoon sergeant or platoon leader as well as the company CP. All his actions could be closely monitored and the marine never needed to feel that he was alone on the battlefield.

So far everything was going smoothly, but Nina would feel better after the first patrols returned about noon. She knew she would feel a lot better with the first set of patrols under her belt. Then a normal routine would be set into motion. Suddenly the radio crackled. It was an urgent call, but not from any of her patrols, but from the Alpha Company CP to the battalion TOC. One of their patrols had captured a live alien.

The battalion TOC was a fury of activity. Cpt. Ben Errington, along with the Battalion Intelligence Officer and the PA, had been summoned to meet the prisoner when she arrived from Alpha Company. The G2 (Intelligence) was coming down personally from the 14th Terrestrial Division to take charge of the prisoner when she arrived. Ben knew he wouldn't have much time with her and this bothered him a little. In fact, he wished that the 14th weren't getting involved at all. Then on the other hand, he knew that Lt Col. Carter would not want to get saddled with the logistics and the responsibility of quartering the alien. Although he didn't like higher headquarters getting involved, he conceded the necessity.

They couldn't bring the alien into the TOC; for security reasons. Even when brought through the Alpha Company lines, she was blindfolded. The Intel Officer set up a clean room where she could be examined without her gaining any information about the unit. The clean room consisted of a tent, with three chairs and a long table. Two of the chairs were for the Intel Officer and Ben; the third was for the prisoner.

The Battalion Intel Officer, Cpt. Mary Paxton, was a tall, handsome Englishwoman with copper red hair and large hazel eyes. She was a no-nonsense lady who liked her coffee black in the morning, her tea with milk and sugar in the afternoon, and her gin neat in the evening. She was as thorough in her preparation as she was frank and to the point.

She brought into the clean room paper maps of the immediate area, of a larger area that included the 14th out to a distance of a hundred kilometers, and a star chart. Not knowing what powers this alien might have, paper was used in lieu of a computer screen. The command and staff wanted the alien no where around its computers. Mary also had pencils and paper, a tape recorder, video camera on a tri-pod, picture cards of drawings illustrating basic nouns, verbs, and some adjectives in order to try and establish a means of communication with the prisoner. Finally, she had some basic need items, such as a blanket, water, and a few food bars.

Dr. Errington, Cpt. Paxton, and the PA with his medical bag were standing by in the clean room when the prisoner arrived. They wore sanitizing surgical masks in the event that the alien carried a virus. Visually terrified, the young woman was shaking when her blindfold was removed. She wore a reddish grey camouflage uniform with dark grey tiger stripes. A matching soft cap with a short bill sat perched on her short, light brown hair. Her boots were as brown as the dried mud that clung to them. Petite, almost to the point of scrawny, she stood no more than one hundred and forty-five centimeters.

When she saw Ben and the PA she leaned back in fear, but as soon as she recognized Mary as a woman, with her longer hair and pronounced bustline, she instinctively inched her way towards the Intel Officer until she was standing almost behind her.

"Well," Paxton huffed. "She has about the same regard for men as I do. I think we're going to get along just fine."

"She needs to get used to men," Ben countered. He picked up the water bottle and filled a glass from the table. He picked up the glass and moved it in a circular motion allowing the water to swirl inside the glass. "Water," he enunciated very distinctly. He lowered his surgical mask, took a sip from the glass, and then offered it to frightened young alien. She withdrew further behind Cpt. Paxton. Mary took the glass, took a sip, and again offered it smilingly to the girl. The young alien looked into Mary's kind hazel eyes. Mary smiled again and held the glass closer to the prisoner. She slowly took the cup from Mary's hands and put it to her lips. Mary nodded and the girl took a sip. It was fresh and cool on her parched throat. She instantly needed more and finished of the water with several greedy gulps. She was given another glass full which she drank just as eagerly.

Ben then opened a food bar, took a bite, and handed it to the alien girl. She took the food bar and looked over at Mary expectantly. Mary smiled and nodded. Without so much as another thought the young woman devoured the bar without pause. It was obvious that she had not eaten in days. Ben gave her a second bar which she ate more slowly as the first one eventually began to make her stomach feel full.

Cpt. Paxton turned to the PA. "Nick," she nodded. The PA approached with his medical bag. Mary gently took the girl by the shoulders and turned her towards the physician's assistant. "Start with the least intrusive examine first," she warned.

The PA took out a palm-size instrument and attempted to put it against the young girls' chest, but she reeled back.

"Here," Mary snorted and she unbuttoned the top three buttons of her own tunic and spread it open exposing her chest down to her cleavage. Nick placed the small instrument against Mary's chest and it sprung to life as numbers began spinning as they recorded her vital signs.

"I can't wait until we get to the gynecological portion of the exam," Nick smiled turning to Ben.

"Dream on, Marine," Mary smirked as she refastened her blouse.

Nick turned to the alien. She finally understood that they meant her no harm. She voluntarily undid the top of her uniform so Nick could examine her. The rest of the examination went without a hitch. Finally the PA took off his surgical mask. "She's clean," he proclaimed. "And she's all yours." He packed up his instruments and stuffed them into his medical bag. "Have fun, guys," he chirped as he headed out of the clean room.

Cpt. Paxton began immediately with her interrogation of the young alien. She wanted to gleam as much information as she could before the 14th G2 arrived. She started by touching herself on her chest. "Paxton," she repeated a couple of times. Then she touched Ben's chest. "Errington," she repeated. The alien touched herself on the chest, "Ngatkuta," she said in a choppy guttural voice.

Mary and Ben looked at each other. "Did you get that?" Mary asked. Ben shook his head. Mary turned back to the girl. "Paxton," she repeated, touching herself on the chest.

"Ngatkuta," the alien said more slowly.

"Ngatkuta," Cpt. Paxton stuttered. Then she held up a picture of a soldier in combat uniform. "Ngatkuta, soldier," Mary repeated several times, each time pointing to the picture, to herself, to Ben, and finally to the girl.

"Soldier," Ngatkuta acknowledged as she pointed to the picture.

Mary laid the area map in front of them on the table. "Ngatkuta's soldiers; where?" she said gliding her hand over the map.

Ngatkuta pointed to the sky and said something totally indiscernible.

Mary again glided her hand over the map. "Ngatkuta's soldiers; gone?" she said as she shot her hand into the air.

"Ngnak," Ngatkuta nodded.

Mary dragged the star chart over the map they had been using. She pointed to Hera's sun. "We are here," she indicated by making a circle with her hand to include herself, Ben, and Ngatkuta and pointed to the ground. She glided her hand over the map and asked, "Ngatkuta's soldiers; where."

Ngatkuta leaned close to the chart and back again. She slowly shook her head. "Hidak maff." She looked at Mary; a painful sorrow filled her eyes.

"I don't think she knows," Ben said.

"Do you think she's lying?" Mary asked never taking her eyes off the girl. "After all, I wouldn't reveal my home to an enemy."

"You're a professional soldier; and an officer to boot. She's probably just so much cannon fodder. I think she would tell you if she knew."

"Hmm," Mary sighed as she turned towards Ben. "Perhaps you're right." She motioned Ngatkuta to sit in one of the chairs and offered her another food bar.

Ngatkuta shook her head and patted her stomach. "Tabi maff." Mary unfastened the girl's left breast pocket and stuck the bar inside.

The presence of Ngatkuta shed little light on the aliens' intent and purpose. She seemed to be as Cpt. Errington had surmised, 'just so much cannon fodder.' She was kept in adequate quarters and given the same rations as the soldiers of the 14th. Her newfound pastime was learning English, which she labored at during practically all of her waking hours and practiced whenever chance would allow. The 14th did not let this opportunity of a willing student, who was also a willing teacher, go to waste. Five of their top linguists were tasked with acquiring what was learned to be the Miurruk language. Step one of a diplomatic solution was in the mill.

Diplomacy, it seemed however, would have to wait. The lateral jumping anomaly was back and the stars began disappearing again; the black cloud and the forces it masked had returned. Fortunately, the marine brigade was on the ground. The 1st and 2nd Battalions had been in place for a couple of weeks now and the 3rd and 4th Battalions aboard the *Saõ Paulo* and the *Milan* had been on station for a little more than a week and were well dug in.

The 4th Armored Battalion was the only tank unit on Hera. It comprised of sixty-five M3A3 Panther tanks. These heavily armored, tracked vehicles had two pulse-laser cannons mounted in dual turrets which rotated on a large central turret on top of a reinforced hull. The two cannons could move simultaneously on the central turret ring or could operate independently on the two smaller turret rings. There were also three vehicle-mounted M12 Pulse Masers for smaller targets that didn't require the devastating blast of the pulse-laser cannons. One each was mounted coaxially beside each cannon giving the gunner a choice of weapons. The third was affixed to an external gun mount and could be operated by the tank commander from his position. The M3A3 had wide tracks so it could easily negotiate snow and mud. It was swim capable and air droppable. Each tank had a four man crew consisting of a tank commander, two gunners, and a driver.

The 4th Armored Battalion included three tank companies, each of which had three platoons with six tanks in a platoon. Each company headquarters had two; one for the commander and a blade tank with a large bulldozer type blade for digging fighting positions for the tanks. The battalion headquarters had an additional five. One for the battalion commander, one for the operations officer and three spares that could be used for reinforcements or for replacement tanks for the companies.

In addition to the line companies, each battalion had a combat support company. These companies carried the special weapons and teams necessary for making the battalions well-rounded combat units. They consisted of four platoons each. An anti-aircraft platoon, an anti-tank platoon, a mortar platoon for providing indirect fire over trees, hills, built-up areas, and such, and finally a scout platoon for reconnoitering.

The Race's defense was a perimeter defense, a large circle of combat forces protecting everyone else on the inside. To make the lines more evenly armed, the Marine brigade headquarters attached one tank platoon to each of the three Marine battalions. To give the tank battalion some infantry support, each Marine battalion detached an infantry platoon to the 4th Armor Tank Battalion. The perimeter defense was complete.

The 14th Terrestrial Division along with its two light combat brigades in reserve and the Marine Brigade were on full alert. In orbit around Hera, Admiral Tony Rodriguez, aboard the carrier, Earth ship *Singapore*, commanded his fleet of the fifty some serviceable Hellcat fighters and the four battle cruisers: the *Hiroshima*, the *Boston*, the *Saō Paulo*, and the *Milan*. The mission of this battle group was to stop as many alien forces as possible from attacking the forces on the ground. Lieutenant General Bob Eastman was aboard the III Intergalactic Corps Command Ship, Earth ship *Bangkok*. He would oversee the battle from space and then ferry down to the 14th HQ when and if the battle went terrestrial.

From his command post aboard the carrier *Singapore*, Adm. Rodriguez and Captain Rita Becker watched the phenomenon the 14th had reported on that initial, eventful night unfold before them. From an ever expanding area out, the stars appeared to black out before them as if someone was flipping a switch. This time, they knew the cause. It was the cloaking black cloud.

"Well," Rodriguez said, never taking his eyes of the black area approaching them. "Now you know what they meant when they said that the stars were disappearing."

Rita marveled at the vastness of the cloud. "How do you suppose they can move that thing and so quickly?"

"Beats the hell out of me, Rita," he whispered almost inaudibly. "We all ready to go?"

"Yes, Sir," she nodded. "The first flight is on deck. The rest are standing by."

Rodriguez switched over to secure communications with the *Bangkok*. "Bob, this is Tony. We're ready."

"Roger, Tony." A pause silenced the radio. "Do you think you can get above it?"

"If we move now."

"Move out, and Godspeed."

Adm. Rodriguez gave the four battle cruisers the command to set sail high above Hera. The hope was that if the fleet could get well above the blanket of the black cloud en route, they could see what was behind it and if need be, attack it. They didn't want to just punch through the cloud in fear of colliding with enemy vessels on the other side.

Simultaneously the five large warships rose above Hera. Like fish slowly floating to the surface of a great sea, the vessels moved ever up, not forward, hoping to reach an altitude above Hera that would give them a clear view and perhaps even an advantage of what lay in store. As they rose, some of the stars that had blacked out reappeared proving that there was a border to this cloud. Ever further they rose until they were several hundred kilometers above Hera. Adm. Rodriguez leaned forward towards the window in hopes of seeing something; anything behind the cloud.

Suddenly, as the fleet rose and the cloud drew near the lights of several large ships and many smaller ones appeared below them. It was a large fleet, an armada. This was definitely not a diplomatic mission.

"Oh, my God," Capt. Becker gasped.

The fleet, too, had been spotted as small fighters erupted from the larger alien ships like swarms of bees. This was the worst case scenario, and it was bearing down on them at flank speed.

"Launch, Rita," Rodriguez growled through his teeth. "Launch the Hellcats."

CHAPTER FIVE

Lieut. Zimmermann's Hellcat screamed off the flight deck as his Flight Black-bat one-zero tore towards the swarm of alien boomerang fighters. Besides their normal weaponry, his six Hellcats bore two torpedoes each, strapped beneath the wings. These ship-killers were designed to penetrate deep into the bowels of a ship and then detonate causing massive interior and structural damage. Placed correctly, they were capable of rending even a large battle cruiser in two.

Black-bat one-zero was escorted by Black-bats two-zero and four-zero. Staving off the enemy fighters they would get Black-bat one-zero as close to the larger ships as possible to destroy them with the large torpedoes.

The proximity warning alarm went off practically as soon as Zimmermann left the *Singapore*. He checked his computer screen and all FIB's were working on his and the other flights' fighters. To the front, more targets than the computers could handle, it was time to go 'Weapons-free, Fully Automatic.' Now was not the time to be shy. They would slam straight through the maelstrom of alien fighters, on to the fat lumbering warships, and deliver the devil's death on a dish.

The three Black-bat flights charged towards the oncoming fighters with pulse-laser cannons blazing their red bolts of concentrated radiation. The cannons were on fully automatic and controlled by the onboard computer, so their accuracy was deadly even at great distances. The interval was still too great between the Hellcats and the alien fighters to really assess any damage and the pulse-laser did lose strength over great ranges, but the small yellow-white flashes far in the distance told the brave Hellcat crews that their weapons were having some effect.

The Hellcats were still out of range of the boomerang weapons which were fixed in the wings like a primitive World War Two fighter. But the high speeds at which the two forces were approaching each other closed the gap within seconds and the Race and aliens found themselves in a head-on collision course. All those fighters couldn't converge on the Hellcats without colliding with each other if Zimmermann kept their formation tight. This limited the number of boomerang fighters that could get a shot at the approaching Hellcats. The aliens fighter design, once again gave the Race an edge.

"Keep it close," Hans Zimmermann yelled over the radio. "It's chicken time. We're gonna punch straight through."

The crews braced themselves as the pilots tightened the Hellcats' formation into a formidable ram's head. Pulse-laser cannons blasting away at the approaching enemy helped carve a hole in the boomerang fighter formation. Zimmermann watched as one enemy fighter after another was ripped open by the tremendous energy wrought by the Hellcats' cannons. The boomerang fighters finally opened fire and sent a hailstorm of yellow bolts of energy their way.

Almost instantly, two of Hellcats were struck by the boomerangs' darts of energy. Black-bat two-four's pilot, one of Mike Boone's boys, took a hit in one of its wings. Under atmospheric conditions it would have been catastrophic, but in space, the Hellcat doesn't use it wings for maneuvering and there is no air to rip the wing away at high speeds. Black-bat four-three was not so lucky. It was hit right in the cockpit and the energized dart went straight through the ship killing the crew. Now it was just a dangerous hunk of space debris hurtling its way end over end towards the oncoming boomerang fighters.

Space debris would be the word of the day as each destroyed ship left in its death finale a trail of ever widening swath of metal, wire, and machinery. This made, at the speeds the fighters were traveling and the speed of shrapnel, even the smallest bolt a potentially deadly projectile.

The Hellcats were playing havoc on the boomerang fighters. They would get hit by one of the Hellcats deadly rays, go spinning out of control and slam into another one of their own ships. Boomerang wings from destroyed fighters were spinning in every direction like maple tree samaras. They were just as hazardous for the boomerang fighters as they were for the Hellcats.

As the Hellcats approached the wall of fighters, small pieces of debris pinged off the aircraft like hail hitting a tin roof. Hans looked back on his left wing to see small holes punched into its skin. They wouldn't be able to land on Hera, he thought. They would have to land on the *Singapore*, away from atmospheric conditions. But he would worry about that when the time came. He pushed the throttle forward and steered his flight towards the center of the gape in the alien defense.

When Zimmermann and his flights punched through the gaping hole in the alien front, boomerang ships began peeling out of formation to give pursuit. Black-bats two and four fell back from Zimmermann's flight in order to intercept the boomerang ships. Hans pushed forward; his flight of six Hellcats still intact. With new or repaired ships and a replacement crew for Black-bat one-four, Lieut. Hans Zimmermann was as ready as he knew he ever would be. Dead ahead soared the alien battle group towards Hera. Smaller ships to the front, emitting some sort of electrical discharged from their bows, seemed to be pushing the black cloud forward. This was how they moved the cloud.

The larger ships were probably troop carriers or capital ships. Either way, those would be their targets. He saw two cigar-shaped ships with large cavernous platforms in the bow. 'Those have to be carriers,' he thought to himself. "One-five, one-one, over."

"One-five, over." Lieut. Yoshiko Matsuo's voice came clearly back over the comms.

"You and I are going to take that big fat carrier looking thing dead ahead."

"Roger."

"One-two, one-one, over."

"One-two, over," Sergey Kracsovichev answered.

"You and one-four take the carrier below and to the left."

"Roger that."

"One-three, one-six. Pick your targets and good hunting."

"Roger, one-one." "Roger, going in."

Black-bat one-zero barreled towards the large ships in the center. Hans knew they would be taking fire from the onboard defensive weapons soon, so he planned to fly in fast, release his deadly ordinance, and get the hell out as quickly as he could.

Aboard the Miurruk carrier, *Tsunggirang*, the task force commander, Admiral Enitir, watched grimly from the bridge as she suspected the bright yellowish white flashes far in the distant to be her fighters being chewed apart piecemeal. The reports from the initial attack on Hera many weeks ago attested to the lethality of this invader's fighters. Enitir and her commanders had hoped that strength in numbers would rule the day, but now she was unsure as she watched so many of her daughters perish in the cold dead sea of space.

"*Admiral?*" from behind her came the voice of Capt. Terparang, the *Tsunggirang*'s captain. "*The enemy has broken through our fighters and is headed straight for us.*"

"*I have eyes, daughter,*" Enitir replied dryly not taking her attention from the fight in the distance. "*Are your gun crews ready, then?*"

"*Yes, Mother*," Terparang paused. "*Admiral, perhaps it would be best if you moved the Command to a less conspicuous ship.*"

Enitir turned to the ship's captain. She looked so young, suddenly; too young for the blue and silver uniform she wore so proudly. Enitir had always loved Terparang's jet black hair and her powder blue eyes. But Terparang was almost young enough to be her real daughter and professional considerations could never condone them playing out Enitir's forbidden dreams. "*You would have me desert my post and go running when first danger approaches?*"

"*Never, Mother,*" Terparang objected politely. "*But I fear this will not be the last battle. Miurruk will need your brave leadership for future campaigns. If this ship is destroyed…*"

"*Hush, daughter.*" Adm. Enitir turned back towards the window. Her own brown hair beginning to grey and aged features of a forty-nine year old lightly reflected in the glass from which she peered. She knew the truth. The fathers had told her. They were spawned from this enemy many centuries ago. Their technology for war was also learned and copied; even improved. But these humans had progressed, if not in space travel, in war even more so than the fathers had predicted. Enitir had heard they were a violent race. They warred against themselves, their own race their entire history. And now they've come to Malerdorn in the Sortreng System to spread their filth. Parasites! Pirates! Philistines! Terparang was right. This fight must go on. "*Ready my barge,*" she said solemnly.

"*Yes, Mother.*"

"*No,*" Enitir countered as she turned and softly put her hands on Terparang's shoulders. "*Today we are sisters.*"

Terparang straightened her back proudly. "*Yes, sister.*"

Zimmermann nosed his fighter straight amidship as the carrier's defensive guns opened up simultaneously. He instinctively dropped down with Matsuo on his wing. Yellow darts of concentrated radiation zipped overhead. 'Their target tracking systems are primitive,' he thought as he led Yoshiko through a series of evasive maneuvers ever approaching their target. He head the muffled pop, pop, pop of his own cannons which could only mean that he had bogeys on his tail. He full throttled with afterburners lighting the path from whence they came.

"Hans. There is some small vessel leaving the carrier," Lieut. Matsuo reported.

"Stay focused, Yoshiko," he called back. "We want the carrier."

"Aye."

Zimmermann locked on to the midship of the carrier *Tsunggirang* and loosed his torpedoes. Two seconds later Matsuo sent her torpedoes down range towards the vessel. Then simultaneously the two Hellcats nosed up at a ninety degree angle, shot straight up for a couple of seconds, made another ninety degree adjustment sending them back in the same direction from which they had approached the carrier, and went screaming back into the fray against the boomerang fighters.

The four torpedoes streaked towards the *Tsunggirang*. Locked on target, nothing short of a direct hit from a pulse-laser could stop them. Terparang watched the missiles jet towards her vessel, the yellow flashes of her defensive guns couldn't stop the oncoming torpedoes.

"*Sound collision*," she screamed, but the alarm never came as the mighty Miurruk carrier trembled and spun from the impact and subsequent explosions within her belly. Terparang was thrown to the deck as emergency sirens blared away. She never had time to regain her footing when the second two torpedoes slammed into the carrier's side. A mighty explosion lit up the darkness exposing the entire Miurruk fleet as the *Tsunggirang* rent in two. A secondary explosion caused by the damaged fuel cells disintegrated the aft portion of the *Tsunggirang* sending the bow end over end towards Hera.

Terparang crawled to the control station there in the pressurized bridge. The lights were still on so she knew she had emergency power. She activated the lateral thrusters to slow the nose of the *Tsunggirang* out of its cartwheeling. There were three other women, two junior officers and a sea mate, on the bridge with her and she wondered how many more were alive in the pressurized portions of the remainder of the ship. She went to the window, her reflection staring back at her. Her blue and silver uniform stained with dark splotches. Terparang looked down. Blood, she was covered in blood. She suddenly felt the throbbing on her head and reached up to find a gaping gash.

Capt. Terparang looked out the window to see the expanding debris field that was once her ship. More flashes lit up the fleet as the second carrier, *Untuknguk*, succumbed to the enemy's relentless assault. Then one of the large troop carriers with its thousands of lives reeled to the torpedoes' deadly blow. Terparang wanted to cry. So many sisters lost this day.

"*Captain, are you all right?*" one of her officers joined her at the window. Terparang tried to wave her off. "*Captain, you're hurt. Come let us tend to you.*"

"*Are there any more sisters alive, daughter?*"

"*Yes, Mother.*"

"*How many?*"

"*We're getting a headcount now, Mother. Please, come, let us help you.*"

"*My ship is gone,*" Terparang sighed. "*What does it matter now if I should follow her?*"

"*We are still here, Captain. We need you.*"

Terparang turned to her subordinate and nodded.

Aboard the Earth ship *Singapore*, Adm. Rodriguez watched the battle far below. He watched as alien battle cruisers came in close to take positions around the larger ships in an effort to afford them some better protection. Their tactics so antiquated, they seemed to be learning from scratch.

Three flights of fighters remained on the *Singapore* for the possibility of a ground war. Six flights were currently engaged. Three Hellcats were left in reserve, possibly to protect the fleet if need be. The air war seemed to be going well, but was it enough to stop the aliens from invading Hera?

"Rita?"

"Yes, Admiral?" Captain Becker joined Rodriguez on the observation deck.

"Get me General Eastman on the horn. I want to send in the battle cruisers."

"Aye, Sir."

With the *Saõ Paulo* remaining behind to protect the *Singapore*, the *Hiroshima*, *Boston*, and *Milan* set sail towards the distant alien armada. One flight of Hellcats was called to break contact and head back to escort the battle cruisers as they entered the fray. There were still many boomerang fighters choking the spaceway between the *Singapore* and the alien fleet.

The battle cruisers came under fighter attack as they neared the battle area. Their weapons were computer controlled allowing a greater percent of accuracy over the aliens. Despite their defensive fire and the fighter cover provided by the Hellcats the boomerang fighters did inflict damage on the ships of war. But the alien fighters had only been armed for dogfights and carried no high explosive ordinance to tackle something as large as a battle cruiser.

As they entered the debris field, chunks of metal, wire, machinery, and now even body parts struck the approaching battle cruisers. They drove on despite the constant hail of debris, some of it dangerously large and some of it dangerously fast, until they were in good range to loose their cannons. Straight ahead were three large vessels, probably troop ships, surrounded by a dozen or so war vessels of varying sizes. All three fired simultaneously sending a barrage of energy that looked much like ball lightening towards the alien battle cruisers. This munition, though devastating in its effect, was less accurate than the weaker pulse-lasers and some of the shots missed their mark.

There were six larger warships of battle cruiser class that returned volley on the Race's three cruisers. The *Boston* took a glancing blow that sent a splash of spark and metal into space. The alien battle cruisers were firing from the broadside so they were able to bring all guns to bear on the approaching ships. Over the expanse of space fiery balls of energized plasma crisscrossed back and forth as the two enemies exchanged volleys. Occasionally two fireballs from opposing sides would collide in mid-flight sending a spectacular flash of light and sparks into space like a large firework's display.

The *Hiroshima* scored three direct hits on one cigar-shaped alien battle cruiser gouging large holes in its dorsal plane. The damaged cruiser shook violent with each blow, sending its brave crew to the deck and keeling it in a lopsided spin. The crew managed to stabilize the large ship, but its guns fell silent. All effort was directed to firefighting and saving what crew they could. The *Hiroshima* selected another target.

The *Milan* was not so lucky. It took a direct hit to the bridge killing all there. All controls were destroyed so it glided helplessly out of formation; a wounded buffalo waiting for the wolves to strike. The gunners fought desperately with the incoming boomerang fighters that smelled blood in the water while others of the crew worked feverishly to bring the large ship back under control.

Inside one of the boomerang fighters the young pilot wiped a tear of hopelessness and frustration away. They were no match for these devils from a distant galaxy; her sisters were dying by the handful, and she saw her world unraveling. She aimed her fighter towards the *Milan* and selected hyper-speed on her control panel. Her onboard computer automatically charted an oblique course around the large battle cruiser to avoid collision. The pilot overrode the computer and set her plane's course direct amidship of the *Milan*. She punched the hyper-speed control and the small fighter bolted throwing her back in her seat. She closed her eyes and whispered, '*mother*.'

The gun crews on the *Milan* never had time to react. The computer reacted in time, but never had time to bring guns to bear on the lone alien fighter. The fighter dashed like a streak as it penetrated the side of the battle cruiser. From the other side a large plume of orange, yellow, and red fire and black smoke erupted leaving a gaping hole that sucked out material and men and women to the cold airless vacuum of space. As intuition drives initiative and initiative drives impulse, within minutes two more boomerang fighters drove hyper fast into the belly of the ship. The mighty battle cruiser shuttered and rolled from the impact and then disappeared in a fiery ball of flame. The *Milan* was lost.

There was no time for good-byes. The *Hiroshima* and *Boston* continued to plow towards the enemy fleet their cannons blazing. This time the *Hiroshima* took a hit and the *Boston* another, but both ships battled on. Another alien battle cruiser limped from harm's way, black smoke billowing from its side.

Despite the efforts made by the Hellcats and battle cruisers, the armada, pushing its mysterious cloud before it, reached Hera and immediately began deploying small vessels of troops and equipment into the black cloud as it wrapped itself around the besieged planet. As the alien battle cruisers and destroyers covered the deployment, the boomerang fighters buzzed around menacingly warding off further attacks. The Hellcats couldn't pursue the landing barges for fear of collision in the black cloud and any damage that may have been caused in combat by shot or debris which could cause a catastrophic failure in the structural integrity of the war birds once they entered atmospheric conditions.

Lieutenant General Eastman ordered the disengagement of the battle cruisers when the *Milan* was destroyed and the *Hiroshima* and *Boston* started taking on excessive damage. They had three battle cruisers left and he didn't want them lost on the first day when there would probably be so many other battles to fight. He had radioed the 14th that the enemy was coming. The Navy had done what it could. Now it was up to the Army and the Marines to win the day. He directed Adm. Rodriguez to start recovery operations, a lengthy and precarious task of finding any live souls trapped in airtight compartments among the wreckage or drifting in disabled fighters all among an ever widening debris field. But they would make every effort to find everyone who had breath in their lungs, friend or foe, and pluck them safely from the cold, black abyss.

Major General Gregory Swanson and Brigadier General Beverly Wilson were standing outside the division TOC and had been watching the show overhead as were so many others in the 14th Terrestrial Division and the Marine Brigade. It started at dusk, just above the horizon where the sky turns a deeper shade of blue; small flashes in the sky denoting the dogfight at the edge of the black cloud. Then a short time later a large flash somewhere behind the black cloud that was so bright the northwest edge of the cloud could be seen clearly for about two seconds. And then another followed seconds after that. But even as the sky grew black and starless from the cloud, the real show was about to begin.

The debris field widened through the black cloud and as it entered Hera's atmosphere, a shower of meteors hailed down through the sky leaving trails of brownish grey smoke behind. Some were from tiny particles that looked like an everyday meteor, but most were from large chunks of metal that lit up the night and left a fiery trail three quarters across the sky. Some pieces were too large to completely disintegrate and crashed down on Hera with loud thuds. The debris shower lasted for what seemed like hours and everyone pondered the fate of the brave men and women up there who were first to draw blood from their enemy.

MG. Swanson was abruptly called to the radio. He returned shortly and merely stuck his head out from behind the TOC curtain. "Come on, Bev, it's our turn," he said dryly and ducked back inside the cover.

Cpt. Nina Errington watched the debris shower from her company CP with much interest. It was by far one of the most spectacular lightshows she had ever seen, but the cost of human suffering to create the show was sobering and doused any enjoyment one might receive. Then in the distance on the horizon she caught a different kind of display. At first she thought they might just be other pieces of wreckage burning in the atmosphere, but the objects started maneuvering left and right. Spacecraft! But whose?

She flipped down the visor on her helmet and turned on the heads-up display which gave her, among other things, azimuth and range readings. Using the built-in communication set, Nina alerted the Battalion TOC on the secure net. "Juliet seven-three, this is Lima four-six, over."

"Juliet seven-three, over," returned the operator from Battalion.

"Lima four-six. Be advised that I have a dozen or more bogeys at bearing two-seven-niner, range three-niner k's, over."

"Roger, Lima four-six. The other units are verifying the same, over."

"Lima four-six, out." Nina raised the visor and stared off into the distance where the lights had gone below the horizon as one of her Marines poked his head outside the CP flaps.

"Ma'am? The platoons are reporting bogeys to the west."

"Roger," Cpt. Errington acknowledged keeping her stare fixed on the point where bogeys had disappeared. "Tell them to stay alert." 'Well,' Nina nodded to herself. 'At least her people were awake.'

Back in the 14th Terrestrial Division TOC Major General Swanson and Brigadier General Wilson were watching as Colonel Yuchi Satake and his people were plotting bogey sightings on the map. Especially in the east and the west, the units were reporting large numbers of unidentified aircraft going down below the horizons. It seemed to the general staff that the aliens were moving to staging areas to prepare for an attack. They weren't going to make the same mistake twice and rush in piecemeal in an uncoordinated attack.

"Bev, let's get some drones out and see if we can get a clue as to where they are."

"How far out do you want them sent?" Beverly Wilson asked referring to their range. The drones had a one hundred kilometer range if the aircraft was to return to its point of origin or two hundred kilometer range if it was allow to keep going until it ran out of fuel.

"Send them out half way," Wilson said biting on his lip. "I want them back. It's for sure we're going to need them in the future."

"What about the Hellcats?"

"No, Bev. I don't want to deploy them yet. I have no ideal if we'll be getting any more." Greg rubbed his chin. "Let's just send out the drones for now."

"Yes, Sir," BG Wilson said and she turned to the G2. "Phil, we're going to have your recon units deploy the drones. Let's take a look at the map."

CHAPTER SIX

Hera was in total darkness; no day, no night; not even a single star to light up the sky. Drones were sent out to try and find the enemy. With the sophisticated equipment housed in the unmanned reconnaissance aircraft, the total darkness was of no consequence and did little to hinder the drones' intelligence gathering capabilities. As the 14th Terrestrial Division awaited the findings of its intelligence units, the fleet, under the command of Adm. Rodriguez aboard the *Singapore*, was busy with search and rescue operations to save as many lives as possible from the unforgiving sea of space.

After the alien fleet had deployed its ground forces, it raced to the other side of the planet and was lost from view. The decision had been made by the commander of III Intergalactic Corps, LG. Bob Eastman, not to pursue the aliens for fear of losing the escort fleet under the command of Adm. Tony Rodriguez. With an ever widening debris field, whose epicenter was not in orbit with Hera, the search for the survivors of the greatest space battle in the history of man become more tenuous by the hour. Any disabled Hellcat crews floating in space in damaged birds or escape capsules had a locating beacon that could be picked up by rescue vehicles from very long distances. Any survivors of the *Milan* would be more difficult to find as each individual would not be wearing a locating beacon. Instead there were emergency beacons in the individual pressurized compartments of the vessel. If any of these survived the horrendous series of explosions that destroy the battle cruiser, fleet would be able to pick it up and rescue any survivors within the compartments.

The fate of any alien survivors was the most troublesome. They had no beacons, at least that the rescue vehicles could locate. The rescue vehicles would search for larger pieces of wreckage; large enough to hold at least one pressurized compartment, perform a risky spacewalk to the wreck, and pound on it with a hammer. If anyone pounded back, rescue operations began immediately. There was some concern that the aliens might refuse captivity and decide instead to shoot it out, but the more alien survivors the rescue ships picked up, the more that fear subsided.

The most spectacular case was of the two alien battle cruisers that were knocked out of action, but not completely destroyed. When they determined that they were not going to be destroyed by Adm. Rodriguez's battle cruisers, they tied along side each other and waited. They could never return home in such condition and they had lost contact with the remainder of their fleet when it disappeared behind Hera. They watched the rescue ships approach and did not fire as these craft were easily recognized as not being ships of war. For the sake of the lives on board, the two Miurruk captains agreed to surrender their ships and the rescue operation began. All together eleven hundred lives were saved aboard those two ships.

When the alien carrier, *Tsunggirang*, was destroyed, the bow section was hurled towards Hera. Capt. Terparang and her remaining crew were able to stabilize the wreckage, but could not stop their uncontrolled advance towards the planet. Using the remainder of the fuel in their thrusters, they were able to avoid death by colliding with the planet and instead maneuver the wreck into a gentle and stabilized orbit around Hera. In her track around the planet, Capt. Terparang was able to witness the battle unfold. She watched as the battlewagons slugged it out and then disengage, neither side being the clear victor. She held her breath as the ground forces were hastily landed on the planet, and she had seen the rescue missions being executed unbiasedly with the urgent mission of saving all lives, friend or foe. So when it came their turn for rescue, she solemnly and regretfully surrendered herself and her crew peacefully to Rodriguez's people.

She and her officers, along with the officers of the two destroyed battle cruisers and any others rescued from floating wreckage were kept separately from the remainder of their crews. Because there were so many prisoners, the ships couldn't hold them all so the alien PW's (prisoner of war) were ferried down through the thick black cloud into the darkness and to the hastily erected holding pens and tents of the 14th Terrestrial Division until proper facilities could be constructed.

Under the supervision of one of the 14th's construction units, the enlisted prisoners not requiring medical attention were put immediately to work building long open bay billets to house themselves and their officers situated at a distant location. The alien officers' compound would be similar except they would be permitted to erect cubicles inside the billets, affording the officers some seclusion. Latrines were immediately dug in the hard Heran ground by the 14th's earth movers and the PW's enclosed them and the washing facilities for privacy.

Water was stored outside each compound in large tanks and then supplied via aqueducts into the compounds. Food would become a problem eventually as the Race would have to share their limited food supply with the PW's, and even though they had the artificial light source to grow some vegetables in greenhouses, not enough food could be grown for everyone as long as the black cloud covered the planet.

The outer retaining fence erected by the soldiers of the 14th consisted of heavy duty wire mesh intended for reinforcing concrete. The inner 'fence' was placed five meters within the outer fence and consisted of motion detectors. Between the two fences, Hera, herself, supplied the escape deterrent; a type of wiry brier with needle-sharp thorns. It grew in long tangled brambles and remained resilient even after dead and dry. It was devilishly difficult to work and could only be cut with strong wire cutters. It was as effective as any concertina produced on earth.

The soldiers of the 14th stretched out the long brambles between the two fences and secured them together end to end and then to the retaining fence with heavy wire. The ground upon which the PW compounds were being place was hard and not easily worked without the aid of pick and shovel. Since the PW's utensils were made of plastic, there would be little danger of the aliens tunneling their way out. Finally, the compounds were under twenty-four hour guard with a minimum force.

The prisoners worked hard along side the soldiers of the 14th. Lights had been erected to facilitate construction. Even though the threat of attack existed, the consensus was the enemy already knew where they were, they had night vision capable equipment, the compounds were not near militarily sensitive areas, and one cannot hammer or saw quietly anyhow. So around the construction sites, large lamps were erected to light up the darkness. However, along the perimeter, at the TOC's, and elsewhere, total blackout was the rule.

Meanwhile the 14th was searching constantly for any signs of the alien forces. If they went to the other side of the planet, they could be establishing a large base of operations like the III Intergalactic Corps and thus would be even harder to root out. The other side of the planet was too far for the 14th under its current configuration to conduct operations while maintaining security at its base camp. It was therefore decided that drones would be launched from the *Singapore* when its orbit put it on the far side of the planet.

While the *Singapore* was conducting rescue operations, the *Hiroshima*, the *Boston*, and the *Saõ Paulo* were in patrol orbits around Hera even as repairs were being made. But all signs of the remaining Miurruk warships and transports had vanished. Speculation was that the alien space force was hiding behind one of Hera's moons. But with all but three of the Hellcats undergoing repairs from the last battle, now referred to as 'The Battle of the *Milan*' in memory of the proud battle cruiser and its brave crew, III Intergalactic Corps did not want to risk anymore losses until they could get back to acceptable combat strength. Besides the *Milan*, the *Singapore* lost nine of the thirty-six Hellcats it sent into battle. Four of those crews were recovered in the rescue operations, the other five crews were considered lost.

Both sides had suffered considerable losses and both sides were out of range from their home bases and resupply. So both sides more or less retired to their neutral corners to lick their wounds and to prepare for the next engagement. The *Singapore* launched expendable probes during several of its orbits but the Miurruk ground forces could not be located. LG. Eastman, Adm. Rodriguez, and MG. Swanson were all growing nervous by this lack of discernable enemy activity. Then on the eighth day, to everyone's surprise, the black cloud dissipated.

III Galactic Corps was in a state of commotion as they, along with the escort fleet, searched the surface of Hera for the enemy. They crisscrossed the planet using every available spaceborne platform that could carry a camera. But no matter which method they used; infrared, thermal, passive starlight, etc., the enemy was nowhere to be found. Then the thought occurred that perhaps they had gone underground or worse yet, underwater. The 14th had set the base camp but a few kilometers from the sea with the thought of eventually building a port. If the aliens had the capability to operate underwater, nothing that the forces had on the ground on Hera was capable of detecting them, and under water the enemy could get danger close before the 14th or 1st Marine Brigade knew what hit them.

Cpt. Nina Errington climbed into the CATV, (combat, all terrain vehicle, pronounced 'cat-v') and the driver sped away.

She was told to report to the battalion TOC. Nina already knew what that meant; she was going to have to transfer command. She was hoping this day could have been put off a little longer, but with the enemy on the ground and attack imminent, she knew the CO, Lt Col. Carter, would not wait another minute.

As the small, tracked utility vehicle rolled smoothly over the rough terrain, Nina gazed out blankly; the passing vegetation, a nondescript blur. It was dawn of the tenth day since the Battle of the *Milan*. Nina had already briefed her company that a new commander would be taking over for her soon. They were naturally happy with the news of her pregnancy, but very solemn about the news of her departure. Cpt. Errington was a good and fair commander who showed genuine concern for the health and welfare of her people, and she would be sorely missed.

Nina jerked an abrupt shiver. The morning mist was unusually brisk today. She crossed her arms tightly around her chest and wished she had told the driver to put the top up on the CATV. A slight breeze jostled the grass and light branches in the trees.

Suddenly the ground beneath the CATV erupted in a splash of dirt and fire, and Cpt. Errington was thrown high and to the rear of the airborne vehicle. She hit the ground with thud. The CATV slammed upside-down beside her. More explosions shook the earth somewhere behind her. A high-pitched hum in the air made Nina look up in time to see a boomerang fighter buzz the treetops at a tremendous speed, its wing guns spitting out yellow darts of radiation at a distant target.

"Oh, my God," she said aloud to herself. "It's started." She jumped to her feet. "Driver? Marine?" she called but no answer. She ran around to the other side of the overturned CATV and there, pinned halfway beneath the vehicle laid the crushed, lifeless body of the driver. Nina stood motionless for a moment, not knowing exactly what she should do next. She was halfway between her company and the battalion TOC. She looked down the dirt road both ways thinking of her next course when suddenly thuds from explosions came from the direction where her company was situated. Instinctively the young professional jumped off towards the shelling; towards her company.

Nina ran down the road from whence she and the hapless driver had just come. Up ahead the thuds grew louder as she drew nearer and nearer to her company CP. She began to hear the clacking sounds of M12 Pulse Masers. Her troops were returning fire; there must be a ground threat to the front. She quickened her pace to a sprint when someone suddenly stepped out from behind a tree along the road and gave her a sharp shove. Errington hit the ground hard and rolled to a stop. Her whole body hurt from the sudden jolt. She rolled over and standing above her were three women in the Miurruk reddish grey camouflage uniforms with dark grey tiger stripes, their guns pointed straight at her face. They raised their guns as if taking aim. Nina released a heavy breath of disbelief, closed her eyes tightly, whispered, "Ben," and waited for the end.

Then one of the Miurruks spoke. Nina opened one eye and saw the woman on the left holding her right arm up in front of the other two women. She knelt down beside Nina and placed her hand on Nina's stomach. She held it there for a minute, shook her head slightly, said something to the other two, then reached down on her utility belt and drew her bayonet. Nina gasped and tried to crawl away backwards, but the two Miurruk soldiers brought their guns back up to the firing position as a warning. Nina grabbed a clump of grass in each fist anticipating the sharp cold blade of the knife in her belly. But instead the Miurruk soldier grabbed Nina's uniform and made about a ten centimeter cut in the fabric. She then shoved her hand inside and placed it on Nina's bare abdomen, just underneath her panties' elastic band. She rubbed it around a bit as if searching for something and then suddenly stopped. The soldier smiled, turned her head to her comrades and spoke. They lowered their guns and both reached down to help Nina to her feet. One of the soldiers searched Nina for weapons while the second bound Nina's hands behind her back. Once they had her secure, they led her back up the road in the direction of the CATV.

As they approached Nina saw several other alien soldiers standing around the vehicle. They had raised it enough to drag the body of the dead marine out. His pants were pulled down to his knees and there was a dark bloody spot on the young man's genital area. One of the soldiers was holding a pair of small oval-shaped objects, each with a long, thick cord looking thing attached. The soldier showed them to her fellow comrades who were showing so much interest in what she held in her hand, that they didn't even notice the prisoner of war behind them. The soldier then opened a case on her utility belt and gently dropped the pair of oval-shaped objects into the case. A cold white smoke, like one normally sees with dried ice, puffed out of her case and lightly floated to the ground. The soldier then carefully locked the case and proudly tapped the front while her fellow soldiers looked on with envy. Nina looked around and noticed that all the soldiers had such cases on their belts. Nina felt herself growing sick as she was marched pass the CATV and out towards the front lines.

At the battalion TOC, Lt Col. Carter examined the map carefully as the place buzzed with the urgency that comes with the unraveling of threads. She got on the horn and radioed the tank platoon attached to her battalion. The breach was in the Charlie Company sector and it needed reinforcing ASAP. She moved the tank platoon and the reserve platoon from Bravo Company to counter the alien assault, keeping in mind that there were still Charlie Company marines in the area.

She glanced over at Cpt. Ben Errington, who was looking anxiously at the map from across the TOC. She knew he was worried. She was, too. Glenda bit her lip in all hopes that Nina Errington got out in time. The fact that Nina was overdue and that she was not at the company CP did not make the battalion commander feel very optimistic. Glenda jerked her head and sucked air through her teeth as she reproved herself for not having brought Nina off the front sooner.

Third Platoon, Bravo Company of the 4th Armor Battalion was in support of the 1st Marine Battalion. Its six tanks had been positioned behind the 1st Marine Battalion's Alpha Company because of the great fields of fire to its front. Charlie Company had some open fields of fire but shared a large wooded area with Bravo Company on the left flank. The tank platoon leader, Lieutenant Mi He ('me-hay') Kim received the word from the TOC to move to the Charlie Company area and engage the enemy. Her M3A3 Panthers were cranked up and ready when the first boomerang fighter flashed overhead.

"Okay, people," she called over the platoon net. "We're moving out to the left; herring bone formation. We'll be supporting Charlie Company. They're being overrun by the enemy. Keep your eyes open, and check your shots; we've got friendlies on the ground. Follow my lead. Let's move out!"

Kim's Panther jumped out of its hide position in the thicket on the knoll behind Alpha Company and sped down the hill towards the road that led to Charlie Company. The five other Panthers roared after Kim as her driver spun the large M3A3 onto the road that headed toward the battle. Her crew was buttoned up; the gunners searching the area ahead and to each side with their gun sights. Lt. Kim was standing about breast-pocket high in the hatch where she could command a better view of the area around them.

Kim's platoon had only driven a few minutes when one of her gunners picked up on his thermal sight some human images in the brush. Kim slowed the Panther down and swung the turret in the direction of the sighting. Suddenly gunner one saw the reddish grey uniforms of Miurruk soldiers and yelled with excitement, "Gun one, enemy troops!"

Kim responded instantly, "Gun one, coax, troops."

"Identified!"

"Gun one, FIRE!"

The coaxially mounted M12P clacked out in rapid succession a fury of red pulses of radiation at the Miurruk soldiers. Almost instantly the second gunner spotted another group of soldiers down the road.

"Gun two, troops identified!"

"Gun two, FIRE!" Kim repeated. And the second coaxially mounted M12P snapped into action. The aliens answered in kind and they fired on Kim's Panther, forcing her into the turret. She had just closed the hatch when one of the Miurruk's yellow darts splashed against the turret sending a spray of sparks five meters into the air. Fortunately for Lt. Kim and her crew the Miurruk small arms weapons were no match for the M3A3 Panther's special armor. The yellow darts' energy dissipated leaving only small pockmarks in the Panther's tough skin as evidence of their striking.

As Kim's Panther received and returned fire in a brilliant display of red and yellow darts crisscrossing paths and a symphony of sparks shooting high into the air like fireworks every time her tank was hit, the other Panthers maneuver around her left and right sides for better positioning to get into the fray. Three of the six tanks exchanged fire briefly with the Miurruk soldiers in the grossly unmatched firefight that ended with seven aliens killed, two wounded, and one surrendering.

Now Lt. Kim had prisoners; a situation for which she was not prepared as she had no infantry with her. She radioed the 1st Battalion TOC and informed them of the situation. They in turn directed Alpha Company to dispatch a squad and a medic to the site to take charge of the prisoners, so Lt. Kim could continue her mission. In the distance, the sound of battle in the Charlie Company area demanded her platoon's immediate attention. The platoon leader could not wait until the Alpha Company relief arrived, so she left one tank behind with the prisoners, took the rest of her platoon, and continued down the road towards Charlie Company. The other tank could catch up after the crew was relieved of the prisoners by the squad en route from Alpha Company.

It did not take Lt. Kim and her five Panthers long to reach the melee in the center of the Charlie Company sector where the forest met the open field. Small arms fire tore through the air as the embattled marines struggled heavily with a large Miurruk force. The Panthers entered the wood from the right and immediately started chopping through the Miurruk forward line of troops. Some of the marines that had fallen back were incited by the arrival of the tanks and took up the offensive to rout the enemy.

This alien unit was better equipped than the squad Mi He Kim and her platoon had encountered before and an anti-tank team inched their way up to a suitable firing position. The two Miurruk women crouched down in a shallow depression behind a tree that hid them from the marines to the front and afforded a little protection from the tanks approaching on the Miurruk left flank. Among the red and yellow darts slicing through the air like a laser show, a bolt of compacted radiation exploded from the wood and slammed into the hull just below the track return rollers of one of Kim's Panthers bringing it to a dead stop. The tank commander (TC) and the number one gunner were able to scramble out just before the inside of the Panther exploded sending black acrid smoke billowing from the two hatches from which the gunner and TC were able to escape. The driver and number two gunner perished on impact of the powerful anti-tank weapon's fire.

The anti-tank team readied a second round to destroy another tank, but the general area of their position was immediately discovered by another Panther which laid heavy M12P fire around their location. They were able to get off one more shot, but under the duress of the Panther's heavy fire, the charge missed and soared angrily over the top of its turret. Their position now positively identified, the Panther chewed up the area with a barrage of M12P fire which ripped mercilessly through the young women and destroyed their anti-tank weapon.

The four Panthers that were left continued their drive between the marines and the Miurruks, their coaxial guns slicing through the alien soldiers. Another anti-tank team made its way forward but was only able to get off one round before being quickly dispatched by a hail of marine M12P fire. Their shot disabled another Panther by shearing off its right idler wheel, but the crew was unharmed. With their second anti-tank team gone and the tanks inflicting severe causalities, the Miurruk women warriors began to withdraw. The marines and the tanks drove them back from the road and into the wood. Because of the trees, Lt. Kim's tanks could not pursue, but with the momentum of the battle now in their favor, the marines were able to drive the aliens back through the woods, back to their original fighting positions, and beyond until it became an alien rout. The company XO, Lt. Peterson, was directed by battalion not to pursue the fleeing enemy, but to reestablish a coherent line of defense.

Lt. Kim's sixth Panther rejoined the platoon after it had turned the PW's over to Alpha Company. A tank recovery vehicle from the 4th Armor Battalion was sent to recover the disabled Panther and her crew along with the two remaining crew members of the destroyed tank. The destroyed tank would be later recovered after the fire died inside it and the risk of any more secondary explosions was gone.

With her four remaining serviceable tanks, Lt. Kim continued to patrol down the road towards the Bravo Company positions. They came upon the fork in the road that led to the battalion TOC. Mi He took one of the tanks with her down toward Bravo Company, while her platoon sergeant took the other tank up the road towards the battalion TOC. Not too far along the platoon sergeant came across the overturned CATV and the mutilated marine. He dismounted his tank. Upon closer inspection the platoon sergeant noticed a large number of footprints made with boots that were unlike the standard issue C.O.P.E. military boot. They had to be alien. He reported the find to Lt. Kim, who passed the information up to Lt Col. Carter's TOC. When asked about the company commander, Cpt. Nina Errington, no trace of her was all that could be reported.

In the 14th Terrestrial Division TOC, MG. Swanson had been watching the developments of the ongoing battle. Somehow they had been taken totally by surprise. Out of the blue, a wave of boomerang fighters shot across the breadth of the division at treetop level, strafing everything in its path, before disappearing over the horizon again. The Hellcats never even had time to scramble before the boomerang fighters made their one destructive swath and vanish as quickly as they had appeared. More as a harassment maneuver than an attack on any one target; the extent of widespread damages caused by that one flyover were still being assessed.

Then came the ground attacks; not a strong single blow at any one point to break the 14th's tenuous perimeter as had been feared, but more like probes; probes to test the Race's defenses, probes in force. They had breached the perimeter in four places.

Four exact places in line with the compass. The attack on 2nd Marine Battalion was from the center of the 14th's base camp exactly along the forty-fifth azimuth. The 4th Armor Battalion was hit along the one hundred and thirty-fifth azimuth, the 3rd Marine Battalion along the two hundred and twenty-fifth, and the 1st Marine Battalion along the three hundred and fifteenth degree azimuth. It all added up to a perfect 'X' on the map. The enemy came in force and penetrated the Division's perimeter in four places and then allowed themselves to get pushed off. That confused MG. Swanson to no end. And then they, too, save the dead and the PW's, vanished into thin air.

And then came the disturbing reports. Reports of castration of fallen men, the capture of men, while leaving females behind, securely bound. It was all painting an ugly picture of a prolonged campaign. Selective prisoners, body mutilation, it sounded like the beginning of a bad science fiction. Worst of all, LG. Eastman was on his way over to the Division TOC to discuss the situation with Swanson. Greg shook his head slowly as he looked down on the floor. This had not turned out at all the way he and Beverly had planned it.

He turned to Col. Satake. "Where's General Wilson, Yuchi?"

"She went to the Marine Brigade TOC to get an update from Col. Hicks, Sir."

Greg Wilson nodded and then rubbed his face with both of his hands. He wished she were here now. He wished he could talk to her.

CHAPTER SEVEN

Nina was led past the overturned CATV and out towards the front lines. They never passed any of her soldiers or those of Alpha Company. She wondered where they could be. As they trudged along the open field past their perimeter boundary, she wondered how the aliens were able to get so close without being detected by the most sophisticated equipment ever developed by man. She wondered why she had not been blindfolded, and then the thought hit her. They probably will not keep her alive, or they will transport her somewhere distant; perhaps even off the planet. Nina grew more nervous with each passing step. The further away she got from Ben and the further away she got from her unit, the more frightened she became. She wanted so much to cry, but didn't dare to in front of her captors.

The three Miurruk soldiers chatted light as they led Cpt. Errington further out into the open field. Occasionally they would stop and one of the soldiers, perhaps she was the leader, Nina thought, would take a small, strange looking instrument, take a reading, and then continue walking. She was the woman who felt her bare stomach. Somehow, Nina surmised, the leader knew she was pregnant. But by just rubbing the stomach, how could she have known by that? And why would she spare her life for that? They were either very human or, Nina gasped to herself, they want the baby. She had already witnessed how insensitive these women could be. Nina began to feel nauseated.

The leader of the group took out the strange instrument one more time and this time, kept it out. She continued to monitor it like they were nearing something, by Nina saw no one or anything. Then the strangest thing happened. The grass beside them began to shift as they walked. Ever so slightly it would shift in one direction and then another. Suddenly, just ahead of them, someone seemed to walk out from the grass itself. Nina let out a cry and jumped back. The three girls laughed, two of them grabbed her by each arm and dragged her forward.

As they neared the woman who had just appeared, Cpt. Errington turned and looked back behind her and saw the most amazing piece of technology she had ever seen. The woman had stepped out from under a large roof held up by long, round stilts. The structure was large enough to hold a mechanized infantry company under it and indeed, that's what appeared to be under the shelter now. The Miurruk women were in full combat gear, checking their equipment, and chatting in groups of various sizes. Nina was astounded. She and her captors had just walked by an entire infantry company and saw nothing but the pasture on which they passed.

The Miurruks had taken chameleonic camouflage to the highest level. The roof of the shelter was approximately seventy-five meters by fifty meters (246 x164 feet) and bowed upwards in a slight arc so inner supports were not necessary. The forward edge slanted nearly to the ground, whereas the back entrance was almost three to four meters tall and could be adjusted to accommodate various types of equipment. It looked extremely light and had to be weighted down at the stilts to prevent any light wind from disturbing it. There were flaps slanting down towards the ground to prevent airborne surveillance of the wide opening. The covering was the most amazing part. Unlike the type of chameleon camouflage used by C.O.P.E. which replicated colors in the immediate environs, this covering replicated form and texture of the grasses, rocks, and other objects it covered. It adjusted to varying degrees of light depending on the time of day and degree of sun and moon light. Since it hadn't been detected by C.O.P.E. forces, it was obviously radar, thermal and infrared imaging, and laser ranging defeating.

Cpt Errington was beginning to get the big picture. The Miurruks move and set up at some distance using the cloud as cover. They erected these camouflage shelters and somehow, that point she had not figured out yet, move them into place shielding their occupants from detection. Overhead and other imaging devices would fail to pick them up and their ground patrols would have missed them because they are trained not to enter open areas; to stay along the wood line for protection and to trust their eyes and sophisticated imaging devices incorporated in their helmets for searching open ground such as this. Undetected, the Miurruks were able to move right up to the Marines' front lines and strike without warning.

After the four Miurruks talked briefly, they led Nina further out onto the field. She occasionally turned and was, from this rearward vantage point able to pick out several such shelters scattered across the open plain. As they approached the far end of the field Nina saw shelters housing boomerang fighters and tanks. Finally she was led inside one of the shelters to a table and chair. They sat her down and gave her some water and waited.

Nina looked around at the inside of the shelter. There were many women working at various tasks. Some of the women worked topless, she noticed. Nina shrugged. In a world of only women, rules of modesty would be different she thought. She couldn't really determine what they were doing, except that she knew it was not to pack up and go home. On the contrary, the Miurruks were unpacking and making preparations; preparations to attack.

Shortly two women walked up, the older one carrying a green bag and the younger one carrying a foldable screen and large square case. After exchanging words with the three, the younger woman set up the screen around Nina, the older woman and herself, and the table. The older woman spoke softly and motioned Nina to strip. At first she hesitated, but she had been treated well so far. The older woman was probably a physician

Nina surmised, and she began to undress. Nina stopped at her undergarments, but the older woman insisted that she take everything off. Nina complied, but she did not feel at all comfortable standing there stark naked in front of these two Miurruks. 'Thank God they brought the screen,' she thought.

The doctor, so it turned out, removed a round disc about fifty centimeters in diameter and laid it on the ground. She motioned Nina to stand on it. It was made of some sort of metal and cold to her feet. Nina gave a short shiver. The doctor then produced a metallic ring from the case. The large ring had a handle and a black box attached to it. The box had several small dials on its topside. Finally the younger woman, the assistant, took a light portable screen from the case. She cradled the sixty centimeter screen in her arms and positioned herself where both the doctor and Nina could see it.

The doctor turned on the ring which made a slight humming sound. She lifted the ring above Nina's head and slowly lowered it over her like a magician performing an illusion. As soon as the ring's plane crossed Nina's head the screen lit up with an internal image of her splashed with brilliant colors. Like a CAT scan the ring gave detailed images of internal organs and bones. The doctor was not so much interested in the organs as she was in the colors displayed on the screen. By turning the knobs on the box, the doctor could change the attitude of the image on the screen. She could enlarge it or even slice it. When she got down to the lower abdomen region, Nina could see the baby arrayed in bright colors. Nina took in a quick breath of excitement. The doctor smiled and said something and then continued to lower the ring past Nina's legs to her feet.

She then had Nina step over the ring with one foot and brought it right up to her groin area. Then with a sweeping motion like a fan, the doctor brought the ring up one side of Errington, over her head and down the other side, providing the doctor with a more or less vertical view. As soon as she was satisfied, the doctor put the ring back in the case and then put the round disc on the table. When she made Nina lie down on the disc, her legs dangling loosely from the edge of the short table, Nina decided that the disc was no warmer to her back than it had been to her feet.

The doctor pressed and poked around Nina's abdomen with large, strong fingers. She then pulled out a small rectangular instrument from her green bag and turned it on. When the doctor laid the instrument on Nina's flat belly, the image of the baby flashed up on the screen that the assistant was still holding in the cradle of her arms. Nina could not help but to gurgle out something that sounded like a mix between a laugh and a cry. The doctor again said something out loud and moved the instrument this way and that to get different perspectives of the embryo. She then removed the instrument and placed her warm hand on Nina's belly, just over the baby. The doctor closed her eyes while she held her hand motionless on Nina's skin not saying anything for a long time. The doctor finally opened her eyes; patted Nina's stomach softly, smiled, and then said very clearly, "Boy."

Lt Col. Carter listened intently to the Charlie Company XO and Lt Kim give their perspectives of the battle, but neither of them had a clue as to what happened to Cpt. Nina Errington. As Ben listened intently on, he imagined the worst. Perhaps she was dead somewhere, or worse yet, a prisoner to those mutilators. And what of the baby? Ben buried his head in his hands and continued to listen to the junior officers' reports.

After the two lieutenants were dismissed, Glenda turned to Ben. "We're doing what we can to find her, Ben; to find all the prisoners." Ben just gazed at the floor. "It may interest you to know," she continued. "Or alarm you; that Nina was the only female prisoner taken. No one's sure why."

"The baby," Ben blurted, still staring at the floor. "They want the baby."

"Why do you think that?"

"Isn't it obvious?" He said as he jerked his head towards the battalion commander. "The Miurruks came prepared today with little boxes for freezing testes. Every dead or captured soldier had one of those boxes on her web belt. And the positions that were overrun; all male KIA's were castrated." Ben jumped up and shoved his hands in his pockets.

"Let's look at the facts," he continued as he paced the floor. "We have a race of, to our knowledge, nothing but women. Sperm banks, if any, have got to be finite and thus dwindling. Cloning can only take it so far because of the time clocks in the cells. Even if the person is using a youth enhancing drug, the cell still has a clock that tells it how old it is. Their race may be on the downhill side towards extinction, for all we know.

"We happen here, and we are considered as intruders. They attack us. Positions were overrun on the night of the very first battle. Miurruk soldiers fell and their equipment picked up by our soldiers. There were no castrations, no little cases of dry ice on their belts. So what happened?

"They come after us again, only this time they know whom they're fighting. Only this time there is a secondary objective; return with the raw material needed to proliferate the race."

"But why would they take Nina?" Glenda jumped in.

"If she's carrying a boy, he would be useful down the road. If they find out she has a girl; I don't know. They have women enough apparently. Maybe they would kill the baby. In either case, they wouldn't need Nina anymore." Ben stopped pacing and looked up at the ceiling; tears welling in his eyes. "I fear the worse."

"Ben, I am so sorry I didn't take Nina off the line sooner."

Ben turned and looked at Glenda. The remorse was genuine; he could see it in her eyes. "Don't blame yourself, Ma'am; I don't," he said softly as a tear rolled down his cheek. "You know my Nina; she would have fought to the end to stay as long as she could."

LG. Bob Eastman sat at the head of the table in the 14th Division TOC; his cup of coffee long cold. Around the table sat the Marine Brigade Commander - Col. John Hicks, the four Marine battalion commanders, the III Corps G2 and G3 – Col. Lillian Ng and Col. Heinrich Steinfeld, the 14th Terrestrial Division's XO, G2, and G3 – BG Beverley Wilson, Col. Phil Smith, and Col. Yuchi Satake, and finally, at the other end of the table, MG. Gregory Swanson. To the side was an easel supporting a map of the 14th's ground deployment of its forces and that of the marine brigade. Red arrows denoted the areas of Miurruk attacks and penetrations.

"Well, from what you have just told me," sighed LG. Eastman as he rubbed the corners of his eyes with his thumb and middle finger. "And from what Tony Rodriguez aboard the *Singapore* has said, there is no way that a force that size could have gotten so close, on four fronts, and caught us all with our knickers to our knees." Bob Eastman leaned forward, his arms crossed on the table. "But they did," he paused and looked at every officer at the table. "Now I want to know how."

Silence filled the room to a state of discomfort. No one had an answer. Finally, the Division G2 spoke. "Sir, I've discussed this in length with my 2's in the field and the consensus is the enemy has some sort of protective cloak that got them within striking range without our detecting them."

"Are you talking camouflage, Colonel?"

"Yes, Sir."

Eastman sat back in his chair. "It would have to be damn good camouflage."

"Yes, Sir. It would."

Eastman looked over at his G2. "Lilly, do you concur with this?"

Col. Ng shifted slightly in her chair. "Sir, let's look at what it isn't. They didn't tunnel, they didn't airdrop, they didn't storm the beaches, and they didn't just walk up uncovered. They had to have approached under some sort of stealth blanket."

"And we can't detect it."

"Apparently not with our current technology." Lilly quickly amended, "Sir."

"Boys and girls, this is not going to let me sleep very well." Bob took a sip of his coffee. "Ugh, cold." A soldier standing by quickly brought a fresh cup. Eastman slowly sipped the fresh coffee, swirling the hot bitter liquid around his tongue as he mulled the problem over in his mind. He cocked an eyebrow and looked at his officers. "When the Miurruks hit our positions, were they under this special cloak?"

"No, Sir," replied John Hicks. My marines spotted them advancing through the morning mist."

"Then at some point, somewhere, the Miurruks have to come out from their camouflage blanket to disperse and move forward." Eastman slammed his hand on the table. "And that's where I want your marines."

"But, Sir. We don't know where that point is," Hicks protested mildly.

"Neither do I, Colonel. But I want you to find it. They are women; humans, almost. Their physical endurance is the same as ours. They came in on foot, then their drop-off point cannot be too far out. Put out some LRRP's (Long Range Reconnaissance Patrol; pronounced 'lurp'). Not too far out; no more than a couple of klicks (kilometers). Have them hunker down for a few days to see if they can pick anything up.

"Greg, I want one squadron of Hellcats in the saddle, engines idle, twenty four hours a day."

"Roger. I'll run them on four hour shifts. Are we going to be able to afford the fuel, though?"

"We have to. We've got to be ready to go. We were damn lucky none of them were hit on the ground during that last strafing run." Bob Eastman leaned back in his chair and finished his cup of coffee. He smiled to himself. They would be better prepared next time.

Back at the 1st Marine Battalion TOC, Lt Col. Glenda Carter briefed her company commanders and battalion staff at an impromptu command and staff meeting. Ben listened intently as she explained the mission. Each company would establish three, two men LRRP teams. The LRRP teams would go out about one and a half to two klicks and find a position where they would have the best field of vision back towards the company. They would then establish a good hide position that would prevent them from being detected. They would stay out three days and then would be relieved by another team.

As the enemy would surely have sophisticated electronic warfare equipment, the teams would report any activity over burst transmitter. This meant typing out the entire message on the transmitter and then pressing the send button. The message would be sent in one electronic flash that lasted only a fraction of a second. This would help prevent the Miurruks from triangulating their radio transmission beams and would cut down on the chance of the LRRP teams being discovered.

After the command and staff meeting, Cpt. Errington requested an audience with the battalion commander. As they walked into the office, Lt Col. Carter shut the door behind them and walked over to her desk. She turned and faced Cpt. Errington and spoke before he could get the first words out of his mouth. "NO! You're not going out on patrol."

Ben was reeled at the CO's perceptiveness and abruptness. "But, Ma'am."

"No, Ben," she spoke firmly. "I understand how you feel. I empathize, but this is a combat mission and you are not a combat arms officer."

"I won't get in the way, Ma'am. I swear it."

"You will be in the way. The moment you join a team, they will look to you as the leader. They're trained that way."

"I'll take off my rank."

"Ben, listen to me. First of all, everyone knows you; they know you're the science officer, so that won't work. Secondly, it's inherently dangerous…"

"I don't care."

"Listen to me. The patrols are just going to go out and sit a few days. No communication, little food, less rest. And then they're going to come back in again. They're just going to sit there. They can't talk; barely move. Actually, the hardest part is trying to stay alert. And what am I suppose to do for a science officer while you're gone?"

"Ma'am, the battalion doesn't need a science officer right now. Maj. Southerland says we're all just a bunch of overpaid eggheads who don't deserve to wear the uniform anyway."

"He said that?" Glenda cocked an eyebrow.

"Yes, Ma'am. And now that we are truly at war, he considers our worth even less. He's told me three times in the TOC to stay out of his way. He doesn't want me there."

"I'll talk to him."

"Oh, please no. That would only make matters worse." Ben Errington paused, his lower lip trembling slightly. "Ma'am. Nina is all I have. I can never go home, not to my own time, the history has already been written. I'm going crazy. I can't concentrate. I would rather be out there doing something to find her, even if it meant sitting in a damp hole for three days doing nothing, than doing nothing to find her back here."

Glenda shook her head. She knew it made sense to Ben and she understood what he meant even if she could have never repeated it.

"Please, Ma'am. I'll do anything you want, I won't complain. But please give me this shot."

Glenda looked into Ben's eyes and was moved, but said nothing. Ben felt hopeless and knew he had lost the battle. He nodded his resignation and turned to the door. As he opened the door, Glenda called after him. Ben turned and faced her.

"Ben," she repeated. "Report to Cpt. Meyers at Charlie Company. I'll inform him that you're going out with the first patrol."

Ben's face lit up and he stood up tall. "Oh, thank you, Ma'am. Thank you so much. I could kiss you," and he turned and ran down the hallway.

"It would have been an honor, Ben," she whispered as she walked to the door. "S1," she called to her adjutant.

"Yes, Ma'am."

"Call down to Charlie Company. I need to speak to Captain Meyers."

"Aye, Ma'am."

Cpt. Errington reached the Charlie Company CP just a few minutes before the mission briefing. Cpt. Karl Meyers had reported to battalion headquarters just before the attack. He and

Nina were to have changed command that very morning. If she had been one hour earlier, she'd be safe now. That ran over and over in Ben's mind. Cpt. Meyers had been assigned to brigade headquarters and was sincerely looking for the opportunity to prove his mettle, but when he saw Ben Errington, he sincerely wished it had been under happier circumstances.

The first patrol came in the CP a couple of minutes early and this gave Cpt. Meyers a chance to introduce Cpt. Errington, although in reality, he needed none. Charlie Company especially knew the spouse of their CO, or former CO, as the case now was.

"Cpt. Errington will accompany you on this mission as the Battalion Science Officer. He will be there as an observer only. All orders you take from the CP. Clear?"

Both Sergeant Williams and Lance Corporal Wu acknowledged. The other two patrols entered the CP and Cpt. Meyers proceeded right into the briefing. The patrol Ben was to accompany was to follow the wood line from the center of 2nd Platoon's position until the edge of the clearing. They were to establish a good hide position that overlooked the clearing.

After all three patrols got their individual briefings; Cpt. Meyers had some general comments. They were to maintain radio silence unless contact with the enemy was imminent. Other radio transmissions would be by burst transmission. No smoking was allowed. Someone must always be awake. "Remember," Cpt. Meyers concluded. "We're looking for a force with a mighty sophisticated camouflage system, so she might walk right on top of you or you on top of her just going out to get set up, so be careful." He looked at his watch. "Go get ready and be back here by eighteen thirty hours. You cross the LD (Line of Departure) at nineteen hundred."

Ben followed his team back to their platoon and got ready with them.

"Don't worry, Sir" Sgt. Williams said as he smeared camouflage grease on his face and hands. "We'll get the CO back."

"That's right, Sir," Lance Corporal Wu agreed. "And we'll get the bitches that took her."

"Thanks, guys," Cpt. Errington smiled. He felt comfortable already.

After the three were ready; their camouflage on, their equipment taped for silence, burst radio transmitter checked, weapons checked; they proceeded to the company CP where they were all checked one more time by the first sergeant. They met their unit guides from each platoon who were to lead them through the platoon lines so no one accidentally mistook the other for the enemy. In Ben's case, it was a sergeant from the 2nd Platoon.

The sergeant led Cpt. Errington, Sgt. Williams, and Wu down to the platoon and through the lines and then suddenly stopped. He turned to Cpt. Errington, "This is it, Sir. Good luck," he whispered and crept back through his lines in the darkness. Ben put down his helmet visor and switched on the starlight scope. Everything in front of him turned varying shades of bright green. It was like someone had turned on a giant nightlight. He turned to Sgt. Williams and motioned to move out. Williams nodded and took the lead, very slowly and very carefully.

It seemed to take forever moving through the trees like this, but they wanted to avoid the open field on their right in case any of the enemy was surveilling it. Each step they took was scrutinized for dried twigs, loose gravel, or anything else that could give their position away. They were careful not to brush up against anything that might make a sound, and they spoke not a word. Every few meters Williams would stop, crouch down, listen and watch for a couple of minutes just to ensure that nothing or no one else was crawling through the underbrush. The uniform, the equipment, and the painfully slow pace had Ben drenched in sweat. Every time they stopped, he started getting cold. He wondered if the other two were getting as miserable as he. Somehow, he thought it would have been different. A couple of hours later, to his relief, they reached the end of the open field.

But Sgt Williams wasn't satisfied there, so he made a ninety degree turn to the right and started down the perpendicular wood line. Shortly he stopped and looked at the woods between them and the field. There about two meters from the edge of the wood was a slight depression underneath the branches of a broad bush. He motioned the other two to stay put and crept low towards the depression. The closer Williams got to the edge of the wood line, the lower he crouched to the ground until he was on his belly by the time he reached the bush. He looked the position over. It was good, albeit a little tight for three men, but it gave them an excellent vantage point.

Sgt. Williams turned and motioned the other two forward. Ben went first moving and crouching just as he had seen the sergeant do. Wu took up the rear. One time Ben's knee accidentally crunched a twig and they froze for two whole minutes just to ensure they hadn't aroused anyone. When Ben reached the depression he moved slowly inside, checking every inch for anything that might alert someone. After Wu was safely inside they spread the chameleon camouflage poncho over their hide position. Williams then quietly laid some leaves on top of that. They were completely covered with only a ten centimeter gap to the front left opened in order to watch the field. Wu set up the burst radio, and quietly typed 'T36 SET.' He turned on the radio and pressed the 'Burst Send' button. In a fraction of a second, the short message was sent in the secure mode. Ten seconds later the message, 'ROGER T36' appeared on the screen. Ben and his LRRP team were set. Sgt. Williams pulled the first watch. Ben was thankful to get some sleep.

CHAPTER EIGHT

The next day saw a steady pouring of rain. Each member of the team took two hour watches. For meals, they munched slowly on food bars. They stretched and did a series of isometrics to stay limber. They watched the field and the wood line, the field and the wood line, and the field and the wood line. Not even any animals were stirring. Ben realized that Lt Col. Carter's words were correct. It was very boring.

But that evening would change all that. It was Wu's watch, but Ben was up with him. Between two hour shifts he had taken enough catnaps to keep him awake even though he was dog tired. The catnaps just weren't the quality of sleep Ben was used to, even though his two companions seemed to be taking it okay.

So he found himself quietly staring out at the same old field at which they had been staring all day long. Suddenly in the middle of the field a flash of light, like a triangular-shaped pane of glass, broke the night's darkness. It looked as if someone accidentally bumped a tent flap letting out the tale telling light. Both men jumped waking up Sgt. Williams. They scanned the area with their star-light binoculars but nothing was there; just the same old field.

"What did you see?" whispered Williams.

"A light," Cpt. Errington responded. It was like, for an instant, the ground opened up."

"But there's nothing there."

"I know. If I had seen it by myself, I could shuck it off as a dream or a mirage due to fatigue, but Wu saw it too."

Williams turned to the lance corporal. "What did you see, Wu?"

"It's like the Captain said, a flash of light, shaped like a triangle."

Sgt. Williams looked at Cpt. Errington. Errington nodded, "Yeah, triangular-shaped."

Williams stared out over the field with his sophisticated binoculars. Nothing. He turned back to Cpt. Errington. "What do you think we should do now, Sir?"

Again Glenda Carter was right. Even though Ben was not a combat arms officer, he was still an officer, and they looked to him for guidance. "Battalion said we were looking for evidence of some sort of high-tech camouflage. We both saw it. I'd say that qualifies. We call it in to the company."

"But what are they going to say when I tell them there's nothing there now?"

"No. You tell them that it appears there is nothing there now, but that the light was genuine."

"But, Sir. What if it was a reflection? It's been raining all day; it could have been light reflected off a puddle."

"Where's the light source?" Ben countered. He was growing impatient. "Listen, Sgt. Williams. It's a sighting, it should be reported. Tell them we recommend reconnaissance by fire."

"What!"

"You heard me; reconnaissance by fire. If we can't see it, but something is there, maybe we can bring it out by fire."

"May I put your name to it, Sir?"

"Absolutely," Errington said poker-faced. "And give them our location so we don't take any friendly fire."

"Aye, Sir." Sgt. Williams typed out the report on the burst transmitter and wrote that Cpt. Errington recommended a reconnaissance by fire.

Lt Col. Carter was straightening up her desk when Maj. Southerland came bursting in. "Ma'am, we just got this sighting report from Charlie Company. It says Cpt. Errington recommends a reconnaissance by fire."

"Let me see the report." Glenda took the message and was reading it when Southerland interrupted.

"Errington is out there?"

"Uh huh," Glenda nodded as she finished the message.

"Why is he out there?" Southerland was getting excited.

"I sent him."

"For crying out loud, Ma'am, he's not up to the task."

"No?"

"He's not even combat arms. He's just a science officer," Southerland spat, his face was glowing red; the veins in his neck puffed out like an adder.

"Do you have a problem with science officers, Major?" she asked calmly.

"No, Ma'am," Southerland defended. "They're okay for looking in microscopes and such, but this is a combat mission. He should've never been sent out there."

Glenda stared him straight in the eyes. "Are you questioning my decision, Major Southerland?" she asked sternly cocking her head to one side.

"No, Ma'am, it's just that…"

"Have you passed this report up to Brigade?" She held up the piece of paper between them.

"No, Ma'am, not yet…."

"What the hell are you waiting for?"

"Aye, Ma'am." Rejected and none too happy, Maj. Southerland took the message, spun on his heels, and disappeared quickly down the hallway.

Glenda leaned up against the front of her desk and stared out into space. 'Reconnaissance by fire,' she smiled. 'Gutsy, Ben.'

A short time later, Lt Col. Carter went into the TOC for an update. "Any more word from Tango three-six?" she asked.

"No, Ma'am." Maj. Southerland replied solemnly. "We just got a message from Brigade though. Division is cranking up all their Hellcats and their going to send a squadron over that area for a recon by fire mission. Brigade is sending a company of Panthers over to prepare for a ground attack in case this proves exploitable. They want us to attach a platoon of infantry to the tank company for support. Ma'am, this thing is really being blown out of proportion, I think…"

"Get ahold of Cpt. Montgomery down in Alpha Company. He can attach his reserve platoon to the tank company. And get a message to Captain Errington with Tango three-six. Let them know what's coming."

"Aye, Ma'am."

Everyone now wide awake, Cpt. Errington, Sgt. Williams, and Cpl. Wu sat patiently while preparations were being made for the reconnaissance by fire. The division wanted to conduct the operation before the early morning fog set in. Off in the distance, they could hear the squeaky metallic rumbling of tanks moving into position.

"If you're right about this, Sir," Williams whispered. "This place is going to become hot in a very few short minutes."

"Remember, guys," Cpt. Errington whispered. "We are on the wrong side of the enemy. We don't fire unless we are threatened; we don't want to give our position away."

The two marines nodded. Suddenly overhead the sound of a Hellcat could be heard. "Put out the FIB," Errington directed. Sgt. Williams turned on the small black box containing the Friendly Identification Beacon and slowly slide the box out in front of their position. This would hopefully prevent them from receiving any friendly fire. Then the three hunkered down in their position and waited for the fireworks, if there were to be any, begin.

They did not have to wait long. From somewhere in the sky, red bolts of concentrated energy rained down on the field in front of them. At first the bolts dashed harmlessly into the dirt, then suddenly, a couple hit metal and the night exploded into a spray of sparks. A large light-grey structure appeared, disappeared, and appeared again; flickering like a light bulb about to blow out. Then its power did die and a large, one-story structure stood all so obviously and ominously in the middle of the field. Suddenly the flaps flew open and Miurruk soldiers came flooding out like ants evacuating their disturbed anthill.

Now the full weight of the flight of Hellcats came to bear on the field, as a hailstorm of red death showered the whole area. The camouflaged shelters began to appear all over the field as they were hit and their generators destroyed or damaged. The field lit up as camouflage flaps were thrown open by fleeing Miurruk soldiers desperately trying to escape the deadly red bolts of the Hellcats. It was pure chaos as the women, some of them half dressed with no shoes, some of them dressed only from the waist down, others wearing only a shirt with panties, even a couple totally naked ran in all directions as pandemonium set in. It was one in the morning. Most of them had been asleep when panic's alarm set them fleeing.

The field erupted in geysers of flame and spark as various pieces of equipment exploded here and there. A huge ball of flame rolled upwards into the sky when a cover concealing a boomerang fighter was hit and the aircraft exploded with a tree shaking boom. Suddenly direct fire added to the display of red bolts from the sky as the company of Panthers had pulled forward to the field's edge at the other end and were firing on the fleeing soldiers. This added to the chaos as women scramble for what little cover there was or for the tree line.

Ben watched the horrifying spectacle as explosions threw women, some dismembered, through the air. Then near the wood line where they were, the flaps flew open to yet another concealment cover as women fled for the tree line. Ben noticed a gurney with a woman strapped on it. He grabbed the binoculars from Sgt. Williams and focused on the woman. Her head was turned away from him so he couldn't make her out clearly. She seemed to weakly struggle against her bonds and as she did she turned her head towards Ben. Nina! Ben jumped and scrambled from their hide position. Startled, Sgt. Williams called after him.

"Whoa, Sir. Hey. Where're you going?"

"Nina!" Ben called without looking back.

"Come back, Sir. You'll get killed."

But Ben kept running. Nothing, no one could keep him from that gurney. He dodged fleeing women, pushing them out of the way. He picked one up and threw her to the side. He didn't care. These were not the delicate creatures with whom he had grown up. These were warrior women, mutilators; they were in the same class as men for all he cared, and at this moment he could easily kill any who stood in his way. 'Now that's sexual equality,' he would later reflect.

Lit up by the light of the explosions, Nina recognized him even at a distance. "Ben!" she called as she struggled with the constraints. Suddenly someone ran over to Nina. As Ben drew nearer, he couldn't make out what she was doing, but Ben could see her working at something on Nina's side. He drew his sidearm and sprinted harder towards her. Nina sat up. The Miurruk woman was unstrapping her from the gurney. Ben charged up to the gurney and grabbed Nina with his left arm and shoved the pistol at the Miurruk woman's head with his right. The woman looked up at Ben and his gun momentarily but continued to unfasten the straps that held Nina's feet.

"Kill her," Nina said sternly. Ben was confused. He looked at the hate in Nina's eyes and then back at the Miurruk woman who was unfastening the last strap. "Kill her," Nina repeated.

Ben looked back at Nina, but her fiery eyes were fixed on the Miurruk. "But, why?" Ben asked. Nina didn't answer; she just stared at the woman. When she had finished, the Miurruk woman stood back, bowed, and darted to the chaos outside. Nina put her hand on her stomach and looked up at Ben with tears in her eyes.

"They took our baby," she began to cry. Ben reached down and pulled up the medical gown she was wearing. A large transparent bandage covered a laser-sutured cut across Nina's belly. Ben turned around, but the woman was long gone. He turned back to Nina and held her closely.

Suddenly an explosion at the far end of the shelter brought the battle back in focus. Red bolts of compacted radiation were striking around them as the chaos outside grew to a fevered pitch. Ben scooped up Nina in his arms, the pistol still in his right hand and headed back out into the bloody rout. He headed straight for the tree line; to try and make it back to the hide position would have kept them in the open too long. Ben wanted to get back to the cover of the trees as quickly as possible. The explosions were close enough that dirt and rocks came falling down on top of them. Ben went crashing through the underbrush as he held Nina tightly in his arms.

They were about ten meters deep in the woods when he stopped to catch his breath. Suddenly, all around them, about two dozen Miurruk women stood up in various stages of dress and undress with their hands held high in the air. Ben groaned. He just wanted his Nina back, but now he had prisoners. Motioning with his pistol, Ben led them back to the hide position where Sgt. Williams, Cpl. Wu, and the FIB were located. Ben held onto Nina while Williams and Wu guarded the willing prisoners. Even as they watched the end of the battle played out, more Miurruk women who happened by joined their sisters in captivity. The Hellcats pulled back as the tank company with the attached platoon from Alpha Company made their way across the field in the clean-up operation. By the time the Marines got to Ben's location, Ben and his LRRP's had collected fifty-three prisoners.

Dawn came and Lt Col. Carter and her S3, Maj. Southerland, were walking across the field surveying the carnage and destruction they had wrought on the aliens that night. In their sector alone, they had routed a battalion-size element and its support. In other sectors as well, Hellcats discovered three other battalion-size units and dealt them a heavy blow. Casualty figures were still coming in but at last count there were over seven hundred dead, several hundred wounded and receiving medical attention, and six hundred PW's. Race casualties stood at zero. (It would later be learned that six Marines captured previously were killed when the cover under which they were being kept was struck by Hellcat fire.)

As they approached the rear wood line, Lt Col. Carter and Maj. Southerland found Ben and his LRRP team. Nina was on a stretcher. She was being checked by a doctor before being moved further while Ben sat by her side holding her hand. A formation of prisoners was being led away by marine infantrymen, and Sgt. Williams and Cpl. Wu were enjoying a well deserved cigarette. When they saw the battalion commander and S3 approach they began to rise to their feet, but Glenda Carter motioned to them to remain seated. Glenda knelt down beside Nina and stroked her cheek. The doctor said she was bleeding internally, probably from being jostled during the unpreventable run to the wood line. She would need hospitalization. A medevac had been requested.

Glenda listened to the doctors words but didn't take her eyes off of Nina. She leaned close to Nina's ear and whispered, "I'm so sorry."

Nina shook her head as if to say it wasn't Glenda's fault. Glenda leaned over and kissed her on the forehead and stood up just as the medevac slowly descended to a landing. Glenda turned to Ben, and put both of her hands on his shoulders. "You made me proud," she said softly with a smile. "Now go with her."

Glenda Carter and her S3 watched as Nina was loaded on the medevac with Ben beside her. The medevac rose above the ground, turned and darted its way to the 14th's FAH (Field Army Hospital). She then surveyed the battlefield. "Cpt Errington discovered the high-tech camouflage, called for and received reconnaissance by fire danger close to his own position, thwarted at least a brigade size attack, was instrumental in routing four enemy combat battalions, and was responsible for the capture of several hundred prisoners. And in the midst of all that, found and rescued his wife, a Marine combat officer." She turned to Maj. Southerland. "Not a bad day's work for a science officer, don't you think?" Glenda turned from him and strutted off back across the field, beaming from ear to ear.

Captain Benjamin Errington was awarded the Silver Star for his clear-headed and heroic actions in the face of danger that day. It was the first combat decoration awarded by C.O.P.E. since the Martian Rebellion many years prior, and the first Silver Star for a science officer ever. Captain Nina Errington was awarded the Bronze Star for her ordeal as a POW and the Purple Heart for injuries sustained during her captivity. There were other awards handed out as well. Three other POW's liberated during that fateful action were also awarded Bronze Stars and Purple Hearts. These men, too, suffered physical injury at the hands of the Miurruks in their apparent desperate attempts to regenerate their race.

Thanks to the quick and decisive actions of Cpt. Errington, an excellent opportunity to attack was denied the Miurruk High Command. The bulk of their forces were defeated and scattered. The next few months found the Miurruks gathering their forces and regrouping. They had gone further out and, with their sophisticated camouflage, were impossible to find. The continent was just too big to recon by fire. III Intergalactic Corps had lost trace of them. But the Miurruks were not giving up; this war was far from over. Now there was more than just the objective of booting these bastards off the planet, more than just gathering a bunch of lousy semen; more than just the desire to get revenge for all the lost sisters that fateful night. Now was the time to get back their dignity and the Race had no idea how deep that vein buried itself in the hearts and souls of the Miurruk women.

No Miurruk woman was ever born on earth, but their forebears were. They were from the fetuses, eggs, and sperm unceremoniously and without regard for the human tragedy involved, removed from earth and incubated by a race of true aliens seeking a cheap and expendable workforce. The aliens, known to the Miurruk women only as 'the fathers,' were very highly developed, to the point that none felt manual labor within their dignity. They needed a work force they could control. Humans were another well developed species in the universe, but so violent. They warred against each other incessantly.

The female of the species was not so warlike, albeit, she could have a cruel and sadistic streak in her. This could be eradicated through gene manipulation. By adding the right genes from 'the fathers' into the human girls, a docile and obedient creature could evolve. This worked for generations. Then it was noticed that the girls' genetic pool was weakening. More variation was needed to strengthen the sub-species.

The fathers went back only to find that the humans had evolved to such a degree that they posed a threat to the universe. The fathers began immediately breeding a fighting force; in case the humans ever ventured this far.

When Malerdorn (Hera) was occupied, the fathers weren't sure who was on it. So they sent a small force of their newly engineered warrior women to evict them. That invading force turned out to be human, something that had always been feared. On the other hand, it brought the male seed they needed to strengthen their slave labor force. They decided to attack in force, not only to evict them, but to get the seed they needed to regenerate their slave population.

The father's filled their warrior women full of propaganda about the humans and offered large rewards for bringing back viable reproductive organs of the males and higher, unit rewards for live male prisoners, the younger the better.

But the taste of war was bitter to the Miurruk women. They had been engineered for generations to be peaceful subordinates. Now they were reengineered to be aggressive and even ruthless if the need be. It turned out to be a reawakening for the Miurruks. They became warriors, but they also became aware of their treatment at home on Miurruk. They were growing to hate their masters each step of the way. A new scheme was developing.

Malerdorn became a new hope for freedom. If they could win Malerdorn, then they could start a new chapter in their tormented history. They would be strong enough to fight the fathers, liberate their sisters from the fathers' tyranny, and start their own world on Malerdorn. They would take male prisoners as the fathers wished, but the prisoners would never see Miurruk. They would be used to proliferate the new people of Malerdorn.

On the other side of Hera, far from the 14th Terrestrial Division, Admiral Enitir had set up a headquarters to continue operations against their enemies. The defeat of the land forces had left her weaker than the Race realized. Distance was their only ally at this point. Enitir knew from past experience that the invaders did not have the capability to launch an attack half a world away. The invaders' capable fighter, the Hellcat, could be launch from their carrier when it was above them in orbit around the planet however, so the threat was always present and always real. Their camouflage was still effective. Even though the invaders figured out how to defeat the camouflage around their own perimeter, that tactic would not work well here.

She had set up two recovery camps not far from the invaders to try and find any stragglers that got separated from their units during the chaos. Those sisters that were found were ferried to their new base here for reassignment into new units. Training was immediate and continuous. The prisoners taken by the invaders was another story. There were too many in the custody with the 14th. Even if the Miurruks could break them out, they could never ferry that many back here before they would be recaptured. Reports were that the invaders were treating the prisoners well so that mission could wait.

The next concern was the remainder of the fleet lying in hide positions behind the two moons. It needed to get back to Miurruk to be repaired and refitted. They had to convince the fathers to send more troops. The more the better. Adm. Enitir would send back the male reproductive material as evidence of their successes, but she would not tell them of any male prisoners. She would send back word that the war was stalemated and to ensure a complete victory, she would need as many Miurruk women, both warriors and slaves that the fathers could muster. Although this statement was in fact true, Enitir's real goal was to free as many of her sisters and daughters as she could from the clutches of the fathers and have them relocated here on Malerdorn.

Without the cloak of the black cloud, it would be difficult for the fleet to set sail without being detected and surely pursued. They would have to wait until the moons of Hera were in the right position that they would conceal the withdrawal of the fleet at least until it was well out of striking range. That would be another three weeks.

Enitir gathered her officers on the ground for a meeting. She needed the pledge of their loyalty to form a new Miurruk government on Malerdorn. She needed them to forsake the fathers and swear their allegiance with her. She was confident of her victory. The fathers were oppressive and an entirely different species.

After the meeting Adm. Enitir retired to her office under one of the large camouflage covers. She stared at the map of Malerdorn and smiled. The officers were all in line, the revolution was born, and Malerdorn would be hers.

Lt Col. Carter was reviewing the latest field traffic (radio messages) when Captains Ben and Nina Errington reported. "Come in, come in," Glenda beamed as Ben rolled Nina in her wheelchair into the CO's office. "How are you doing, Nina? Sit down, Ben," Glenda said. "Would you two like some coffee?"

"That would be great," Ben replied as Nina nodded. Glenda went to the door and instructed the Adjutant to have someone bring in some coffee. A lance corporal brought in a tray with three mugs and offered them around.

"I know you are curious as to why I brought you here," Glenda began. Ben and Nina nodded at each other and gave their attention back to the CO. "Ben, I know you feel that you've been rewarded enough for your actions during the Night of the Big Rout." Ben nodded. "Well, communication travels slow over great distances and 5th Frontier Fleet has only recently gotten word of the battle and your participation in it." Glenda paused. "Needless to say, they were impressed. So impressed they reviewed your entire personal record jacket." Ben cocked his head, not sure what to expect next. Nina held her breath, and the colonel smiled. "Ben, you've been field promoted to the rank of major."

"Yes!" Nina shouted, jumping half way out of her wheelchair.

Ben was speechless. Glenda offered her hand in congratulations and Nina offered a hug and a kiss.

"The promotion ceremony will take place at the 14th Division TOC tomorrow."

"Must it take place there?" Ben objected mildly.

"The brass is proud of you, Ben. Give them the chance to show it.' Glenda waved her hands in the air as if dismissing the topic. "Ben, that is not the only reason I called you here. As a major you cannot remain here as the science officer. You have to be either transferred or given a position commensurate with your rank." Glenda paused. "Ben, I want to make you my S3."

Nina bounced up and down in her chair for joy and Ben's jaw dropped. "Ma'am, I'm not a combat arms officer."

Again Glenda waved off the objection. "That's not a problem, Ben. If it were my job or one of the line company commander's jobs, that would be an issue. As for my staff, I have a lot of say as to who I want where."

"Ma'am, I don't think I'm qualified."

"Listen, Ben. You have already proven yourself. The brigade commander himself approved the move. I'm not asking you to lead an attack up a hill. I've got good line officers to do that. I need a thinker who can make a good snap decision when the pressure is on. I've seen you do that. You level-headed, you care, and you're a professional. I want someone who can think on his feet and is not afraid to make a decision. You've got that quality, Ben. What do you say?"

"What about Maj. Southland?"

"Oh, he's being offered a new job in a higher headquarters. Don't worry about that, that's my job."

Ben looked over at Nina. The big smile on her face showed approval. She was so proud. "Well," he hesitated. "Yes, Ma'am. I'll give you my best."

Glenda smiled and offered her hand, "I know you will. I look forward to working with you. Now if you two will excuse me, I have some more business to tend to."

As Ben and Nina were leaving, Maj. Southerland was coming in. He looked at them warily as they passed and then entered the CO's officer. "You wanted to see me, Ma'am?"

Lt Col. Carter turned around and handed him a piece of paper. "Congratulations, you're being moved up." She waited patiently as he read the orders.

"Ma'am, these orders assign me to the G3 section at III Corps."

"Yes, you'll be working for Col. Steinfeld; he's a good man. I know you will learn a lot."

"But, Ma'am. This is a pencil pusher's job."

"I know you will do a good job, Major."

"But Ma'am," Southerland whined as his arms feel limp by his side.

"I'm sure you will make us proud. Will there be anything else, Major?"

CHAPTER NINE

The next few weeks saw a relative calm in and around the 14th's perimeter. Patrols were being sent out to try and locate the Miurruk forces but, except for a straggler captured here and there, no enemy units were found. This lack of activity actually concerned the leadership of the III Intergalactic Corps and 5th Frontier Fleet more than if contact had been made.

The first group of settlers had arrived at Hera and was ferried down to start building their civilization. True to custom, they gave the settlement, centered around the 14th's base camp, its name. It was to be called Athenaburg; Athena after the Greek virgin goddess of wisdom, fertility, war, and handicraft and burg after the German word for castle to commemorate the armed struggle that was its humble beginnings.

The first group of settlers was configured to set up industry on Hera, so their space convoy included much of the machinery and skilled craftsmen required to establish an industrial base. Unfortunately, because of the war on Hera, the first priority of that industry was relegated to outfitting and maintaining its new army.

The first group of settlers numbered around thirty-five thousand men, women, and children. Most of the young men and many of the young women had enlisted into a self-defense force upon learning of the war on their new planet and were trained by a C.O.P.E. cadre en route. They formed the 1st Infantry Division (1st ID) of the Hera Volksarmee; the first indigenous armed forces on the new planet. At ten thousand strong, they were a formidable force.

With a combat division now on Hera, some of the tension was off the 14th Terrestrial Division and the 1st Marine Brigade. A new perimeter was formed around Athenaburg that stretched all the way to the sea, now called The West Sea. The 1st Marine Brigade was positioned around the eastern portion of the oblong perimeter. This was the area where much of the previous fighting had taken place. The Volksarmee's 1st Division positioned their 1st Infantry Brigade along most of the northern perimeter boundary and the 2nd Infantry Brigade along the southern perimeter boundary which included a long stretch of the Saint Ursula River. The 3rd Infantry Brigade positioned one battalion on the far western end of the northern boundary from the 1st Brigade to the sea and one battalion on the St. Ursula River from the 2nd Brigade to the sea and the final battalion along the coast. This effectively boxed in Athenaburg and a sizable portion of land for development.

The III Intergalactic Corps established its permanent headquarters in Athenaburg where it retained control of the military forces both on the ground and in space. The 14th Terrestrial Division resumed its mission of research and construction. Its 1st Light Combat Brigade had the mission of guarding the Miurruk prisoners and the 2nd Light Combat Brigade took up civil law enforcement until the new Hera populace could firmly establish its own civil governing and law enforcement base.

Adm. Rodriguez's people had it the worst. The original intent was for the warships to stand down allowing the crews to relax on the new planet. But with the ever constant threat from space looming, the warships had to remain on patrol. This meant prolong time in space for already space weary seamen and women. The best that could be done for them was to rotate small portions of the crews down to Athenaburg for shore leave.

Much attention was placed on the two thousand Miurruk captives, both officers and enlisted. English lessons were the first priority. At the same time, a cadre of translators, both military and civilian, was becoming fluent in learning Miurruk. History and cultural classes began to enlighten the Miurruk women about the Race and indeed their own past. And the Race was taking pains to learn as much about the Miurruk as possible.

The Race paid keen attention to each and every Miurruk and if any showed signs of willfully adopting their new environment and accepting the people from earth, they were put into special classes to help speed the acclimation and indoctrination processes in an effort to fully integrated them into the new Heran society. Many were readily joining the civilian workforce, and many found the newly learned custom of dating exciting, yet precarious. The Miurruk women were naive to the ways of men, but they formed many friendships with the women from earth who took them under wing and protected them from wolves and philanders. It became a self-induced Miurruk custom: First a girlfriend, then a boyfriend.

The indoctrination process was turning out to be more successful than C.O.P.E. or the Herans could hope. Many Miurruk women readily shed their Miurruk way of life and allegiance for that of the earthlings as easily as they shed their uniforms for Heran dresses. And why wouldn't they? They were after all mostly human except for a fraction of one percent. The fathers were totally alien and could be cruel taskmasters. And many were finding love with men, which seemed somehow very natural.

On the other hand, there were staunch Miurruk patriots that would sooner die than take off the uniform. They despised the women who went over to the other side and considered them despicable traitors. They refused to learn English and ignored any type of training that was given them. These remained under the tightest security. This was particularly true of the officers, and the higher the rank, the more resistant they tended to be. A few officers did switch over though, and these proved most beneficial in learning the Miurruk military and its equipment.

The sophisticated camouflage covers remained a mystery. It was their technology, but the Miurruks had trouble explaining how it worked, or the Race had trouble understanding how it worked. Although some working covers had been captured, III Intergalactic Corps was reluctant to use them. If the Miurruks could develop the technology, then they knew how to defeat it. It would be a fool's paradise for the Race to use them thinking they could not be seen. III Corps stuck with their own equipment.

Nina Errington spent much of her convalescence with the Miurruk women. She had a love/hate relationship for them. She liked them because, for the most part, they were like any other woman. She hated them because they ripped out her baby and her uterus to boot. Now she not only lost her baby, but her capacity for having any others. There was the chance of growing another uterus through stem cell technology; it had been done before, but not on Hera, not yet. She would just have to wait.

Nina would spend her time with those going through the indoctrination. They were the most sociable and eager to learn; almost like children. She wanted to learn all about them and their ways. She started language lessons and watched and mimicked things they said and did. She would eat with them, study with them, and play games with them, anything to learn the Miurruk psyche.

She noticed that their washing area was different than what she had experience. In the washroom there was a large tub filled with warm water and some leaves and twigs of plants floating on top that gave the water a soft aroma. The women would sit facing the tub and with large dippers fashioned from a gourd-like plant pour the scented water over themselves. There was no soap as such, but each girl looked and smelled clean. Then they would towel off and, time permitting, recline on a bed of fist-size rocks.

One day, Nina thought she would give it a try. She went into the bath the same as the Miurruk women and stripped down to the bare skin. She found herself a spot at the tub and took one of the dippers hanging on the tub. She dipped some of the warm scented water and poured it over her head. The water felt great. It was so soothing and refreshing, she didn't want to stop. She let the warm water cascade down her bare skin. But something wasn't right. She felt a presence behind her.

Nina turned around to find three Miurruk women standing above her. She jumped up, the ladle held firmly in her right hand. But the women just looked at her and then down at the scar that ran across her belly, just below the navel. One of the girls ever so slowly reached out her hand and touched the scar. She held her hand on the scar for some seconds and suddenly recoiled with a gasp. She looked at Nina and shook her head saying she was sorry, over and over. A second girl reached her hand out and after a few seconds, jerked it back in horror. She just stood there with her face buried in her hands. Soon every girl in the bathhouse was standing in front of Nina touching her scar. Some jerked and went away with their hands over their mouths, a couple cried, some simply withdrew staring at the ground. Somehow, Nina could tell, the young women knew the significance of the scar as if the scar had talked to them. By touching Nina's scar, it was as if they all shared the ordeal and empathized with her. Nina felt the kinship between them growing and the hate slowly evaporated from inside her heart.

The lull in the fighting gave the people hope that the hostilities might in fact be over. They started in earnest building their community and working the land. They began to cultivate some of the edible plants native to Hera and to raise some earth crops seeds they had brought with them on the journey. As Athenaburg was situated near the equator, the Race enjoyed four growing seasons.

Edward O. Bast

In the country the Herans used adobe bricks that they fired in large kilns for many of their farm or ranch homes. They used wood and adobe to house in the brick to insulate the interior from the warm Hera sun. This gave the Athenaburg countryside a Tudor look.

They had the advantage of building the city of Athenaburg from scratch so the city fathers planned it with convenience of movement as well as beauty. They planned the center to be a huge circle with four long boulevards radiating out like the points of a large compass. Cross streets would consist of an expanding series of four rings. This would all be enclosed in a diamond formed by four more boulevards which converged on the four radial main thoroughfares. From the diamond out, all streets would form normal square city blocks.

In the center circle would be a large park with a man-made lake using the fresh water from the St Ursula River. On the outside of the first ring would be cafes and restaurants, none of which could be more than one story high. The second ring would consist of museums, art galleries, and shops each of which would stand two stories. On the third ring and fourth ring would be for more businesses with buildings that were three and four stories respectively. This was to give the intercity a bowl-shape. Outside the rings, starting at the diamond-shaped boulevards would stand the skyscrapers that would house the apartments and businesses. Factories would be built outside the city. The airport also some distance away to the north of the city. It was the intent of the founding fathers to keep Athenaburg clean and beautiful, the gateway to Hera.

Admiral Enitir was informed of the new wave of invaders and the crossing over of many of her sisters by the network of intelligence agents in the field. She was infuriated by the reports and slammed her fist on the desk. The middle aged woman stood up and walked over to the map of Malerdorn on the wall. She knew that she must act quickly if she were ever to have Malerdorn as her own.

But she was not ready and she hated to do anything ill-prepared. Time was never on the Miurruk's side it seemed to her. Adm. Enitir had managed to scrape together enough warriors to make two battalions, but that was not enough to face the reinforced invaders on the ground at Athenaburg. Enitir would have to do something a little more unconventional, and unconventional warfare was what she needed.

Adm. Enitir called forth her staff and commanders. She wanted to start guerrilla warfare against the invaders until reinforcements arrived. She wanted to stop the building of this city the invaders are calling Athenaburg. Enitir wanted farming disrupted, industry destroyed, and the invaders enslaved. The men she needed to regenerate the Miurruk race, the women, too, could be bred to increase their numbers.

"*Wouldn't we be better off to make peace with the invaders?*" one of her officers asked.

Enitir stared at the outspoken woman sternly. "*Daughter, need I remind you of the bloodshed these murdering invaders have wrought?*"

"*That's because we attacked them,*" another officer rebutted.

Enitir turned to her executive officer, Capt. Agnnatuk, in disbelief of what she was hearing.

Capt. Agnnatuk sighed. She was about to stick her neck out for the sake of reason. "*Mother, they have the means to build Malerdorn into an industrialized world in the quickest fashion. We do not. Even with all our sisters here, it would take us years to develop what they already have in place. They are already taking ore from the ground and forging plowshares. It would take us years to get to the point that we could build such a foundry.*

"*Our agents in the field have heard of more convoys coming. This isn't going to stop. They already have us outnumbered and that's not counting the sisters that have crossed over. Wouldn't it be better to marry them, instead of taking their seed and offspring by force?*"

"*What's wrong with you, women?*" Enitir screamed as she looked over her officers and staff. "*Don't you realize we will just be trading one master for another? So what if we don't have foundries? Can we not work the land by hand?*" Enitir walked over and placed her hand on the map.

"*This is everything we've ever hoped for*," she continued. "*It is the end of our captivity. I would rather be an austere landowner here, then a slave to a rich one over there somewhere.*"

"*It's a big planet, Mother*," another officer tried. "*Surely we could share.*"

"*You don't know their history*," Adm. Enitir yelled pointing off into the distance. "*The fathers showed me. They take every bit of land they can from the weak. They will make treaties and promise us things; then, when they have decided they need our land, they will come and conquer us without mercy. Why do you think they come so well armed*," she spit.

Adm. Enitir walked behind her desk and planted both fists firmly on the surface, using her arms to support herself as she leaned towards her women. "*Daughters*," she paused. "*Sisters, I will not raise a hand against any of you. But if you will not help me fight the enemy, then I count you among the enemy, and I don't want you in my camp. Go to your units. Tell your sisters what I have told you. If there are any among them or among yourselves who will not see us through this course; I want you out of my camp by noon tomorrow. Leave your weapons here for those of us that want to fight and go surrender to the invaders. Questions? Noon tomorrow, ladies, after that it's treason. Dismissed.*"

As the officers and staff got up to go, Adm. Enitir sat down at her desk and buried her face in her hands. She felt the weight of the universe on her shoulders. How could she wage any campaign without the support of her own officer corps? She looked up to find Capt. Agnnatuk still sitting in her chair.

"*What do you want, daughter?*" she sighed.

Enitir and Agnnatuk were the same age; forty-nine. They had graduated from the same class and rose through the ranks together. Enitir was a little luckier and got her star before Agnnatuk; other than that, they were about the same. They had always been very close.

Agnnatuk rose, walked over behind Enitir, and began massaging her shoulders. Enitir leaned back in her chair welcoming Agnnatuk's strong fingers. She tilted her head back so she could look into Agnnatuk's large blue eyes. "*Do you think I'm wrong, sister?*"

Agnnatuk smiled. "*I think you are sincere in your belief, sister. But I'm not sure about your methodology.*"

"*How so?*"

"*Our scouts and our spies have seen some of the sisters who have crossed over with some of the young invaders.*"

"*Hmmm,*" sighed Enitir. "*What did they report?*"

"*The men act like lovesick schoolgirls. Our sisters lead them around like pets.*"

Enitir coughed out a chuckle.

"*I tell you, sister,*" Agnnatuk said as she ran her hands down the front of Enitir's uniform and firmly squeezed her breasts. "*We can conquer these invaders in the bedroom.*"

The next morning Adm. Enitir and Capt. Agnnatuk watched as two shuttles with about two dozen women who were not up to the fight departed the camp. Among them rode three officers who had lost the will to fight for something in which they no longer believed.

"Do you think they'll give us away?" Adm. Enitir asked her XO.

"I don't want to think so," she sighed. *"But we must assume that at least one of them will. I recommend we move camp."*

"How long will it take them to reach Athenaburg?"

"I instructed the driver to go slow; about ten hours."

"Let's break camp then," Enitir said rubbing the back of her neck. *"Leave someone back to tell the shuttle drivers where to link up with us."*

"Aye, Mother."

Maj. Ben Errington was in the Battalion TOC going over message traffic when a flash call came in from one of the companies. Ben went over to the RTO (Radio/Telephone Operator) who handed him the phone.

"This is Whiskey zero-three," he said using the S3 call sign for the day.

"This is Zulu two-niner. We've got two enemy vehicles to our front. Shall we open fire?"

"Are they tanks?"

"This is Zulu two-niner. Negative." There was a short pause. "They look more like, I don't know; shuttles."

"Are they aggressing?"

"That's a negative, Whiskey zero-three. They're just sitting there."

"Zulu two-niner, this is Whiskey zero-three. Do not fire. I say again, do not fire. Do not fire unless fired upon. I'm en route."

"This is Zulu two-niner, roger."

"Whiskey zero-three, out." Maj. Errington handed the phone back to the RTO and grabbed his helmet. "Where's my translator?" he called as he gathered his combat gear.

"Here, Sir," came the voice of Ngatkuta, the young alien who was the first to be captured and the first to cross over. She had been assigned to 1st Battalion headquarters as a civilian translator after her English had reached the proficiency level deemed usable by III Intergalactic Corps.

Ben turned to his assistant S3. "I'm going down to Alpha Company. They got a couple of enemy vehicles to their front. I'm going to go check it out."

"Yes, Sir."

Ben grabbed Ngatkuta and jumped into a CATV. The driver raced them to the Alpha Company CP where they met Cpt. Montgomery. He led them to one of the 3rd platoon's positions, where, sure enough, two shuttle-like vehicles sat in the middle of an open field.

Ben handed Ngatkuta a megaphone. "Ngatkuta, asked them to drop their weapons and exit the vehicle. Tell them no harm will come to them. Brian, have your people hold their fire."

Ngatkuta spoke into the megaphone in Miurruk. Shortly the women warriors started climbing out of the two vehicles one by one. Maj. Errington and Ngatkuta went out to meet them. Everyone, except the two drivers, was unarmed. They explained their desire to cross over and how their command had condoned it.

Ben called battalion and brigade to have some transport come out and pick up twenty-six PW's for indoctrination. He then called Lt Col. Carter direct and explained the situation. He then added a recommendation. Again it was gutsy and would take some higher level decisions, but she would give it a shot. Besides everyone in the command knew Ben Errington now and held him in high regard. If anyone could pull this off, it would be Ben.

The Miurruk shuttle drivers were anxious to head back, but Ben and Ngatkuta were able to convince them to linger and have some supper while the wheels at III Corps were turning. Shortly the shuttles pulled up for the twenty-six new PW's, but when the doors opened, twenty-six of the hardcore Miurruks who refused to cross over, mostly officers, exited the vehicles first. Among them was the captain of the *Tsunggirang*, Capt. Terparang.

As a goodwill gesture, Ben felt if, in return for those who wanted to cross over, they exchanged the loyalist that perhaps, just perhaps, negotiations with the Race would be considered practical by the Miurruk command.

It was a solemn crossing in the field in front of Alpha Company. The three officers that were among the crossovers held their heads low as they passed the loyalists on their way to the shuttles. There was much contempt in the air for the crossovers, and Ben wished he had executed this a different way. The loyalists were given one meal and some water. They silently boarded the shuttles and were gone.

The following day the shuttles linked up with the new Miurruk base camp with its cargo of repatriated prisoners. There was much celebration in the camp as humble as that celebration was under the circumstances. Adm. Enitir welcomed her sisters back and then took the repatriated officers and Capt. Agnnatuk into her office. They gave her a full debriefing of their capture and their treatment by the invaders. Actually they felt that they were well treated. Despite that they did not collapse under the brainwashing to which the invaders subjected them. Adm. Enitir listened intently to each of the officers' stories and said nothing until the last woman had finished her report. And then she stood up and paced back and forth in front of her desk.

"*Sisters,*" she began looking at the floor in front of her feet. "*Yesterday I sent a couple of dozen sisters who were not up to the mission packing to the invaders. For some reason, which I must admit, presently escapes me, they returned twenty-six of my best officers and women.*" She looked at the women, "*Sisters, I cannot tell you how elated I am. This worked out better than I had ever dreamed. I thought I was only getting rid of deadwood, but I am rewarded by my actions by the invaders sending me my best warriors.*

"*The reason I sent those sisters packing was because they could not believe in my dream. The desire to rout the invaders from their homestead, use them to strengthen our numbers, break completely away from the fathers on Miurruk, and make Malerdorn our new and permanent home,*" she pointed to the map of the planet. "*Those twenty-six you passed yesterday in the field were not willing to fight the invaders. On the contrary, they suggested we join them in a type of peaceful coexistence on Malerdorn. Now I ask, sisters, what say you?*" she said pointing at her officers.

The officers jumped up, their fists in the air, "*Fight! Fight!*"

Adm. Enitir looked over at Capt. Agnnatuk. The XO smiled slightly, gently nodding her head.

Back at III Intergalactic Corps Headquarters LG. Eastman, Colonels Ng and Steinfeld, and Maj. Southerland were awaiting word from the *Singapore* high overhead and almost half way around the planet. Then through a patch via satellite, the word came in. The *Singapore* had the location of the Miurruk base camp.

"Congratulations, Maj. Southerland, your idea worked," LG. Eastman said. "Although I'm not sure planting tracking devices in the PW's clothes is what Maj. Errington had in mind."

"Aw, Sir," Southerland smiled. "Maj. Errington is just a science officer. It takes combat arms officers to capitalize on an opportunity like this."

"Hmmm," Eastman sighed. "How did you do it?"

"We planted the devices in their clothes during a routine search before loading them on the shuttle," he smiled; his chest puffed out. "Real smooth," Southerland bragged. "Real smooth."

"Sir," Col. Steinfeld broke in. The *Singapore* wants to know what to do."

Bob Eastman looked around at his officers. Something didn't seem right, but he couldn't figure out what. As much as he hated to admit it, he wished Maj. Errington were there just to hear his thoughts. Finally he turned to Col. Steinfeld and ordered, "Attack!"

CHAPTER TEN

Lieut. Hans Zimmermann led his flight of six Hellcats off the *Singapore* and slowly descended towards the surface of Hera. It was midday on the Miurruk side of the planet and the Hellcats would not even have the benefit of night to help cover their approach. Zimmerman's Black-bat one-zero was being followed by Black-bats four-zero and six-zero. They had no special weaponry this trip, their onboard cannons would be sufficient. The Hellcat crews had been looking for another chance to bring some death and destruction on the Miurruks and their chance was finally at hand.

They kicked on the reverse thrusters as they entered Hera's atmosphere. The last thing they wanted was to look like eighteen roman candles streaking across the sky on their approach. They wanted to 'come in all quiet like so as not to arouse their quarry,' as one of the pilots had put it. So slowly they descended over what was first a large continent along an approach path calculated by their computers to bring them in on target.

The continent grew larger as the planes approached. Soon the oceans could no longer be seen and mountains began taking shape. River banks grew more colorful and fields and mountains gained more texture. Shortly they were able to distinguish trees and other objects on the ground. Their proximity lights started blinking and they knew they were entering the target area.

Adm. Enitir was discussing possible engagement scenarios with her officers when a sudden bolt of red energy slammed on the ground right outside her cover. The next one was more accurate and entered the cover with a blinding flash, sending sparks and officers flying. Red bolts of death were dropping all in on them with devastating results and the women scrambled over themselves to find the best exit out of the collapsing cover.

A moment of relief arrived when a dozen boomerang fighters came screaming in, their guns blazing. The Hellcats were caught off guard and diverted their attention to the boomerang fighters, but not before two Hellcats slammed into the ground, their crews never having the instant of a chance to punch out.

The boomerang fighters flew straight out of the engagement area and over the horizon leaving the remaining sixteen Hellcats to continue chewing up the ground in the vicinity, a reconnaissance by fire technique, to see if there were any more sophisticated camouflage covers on the ground. They found only two.

The Miurruk officers ran into the cover of the trees but the Hellcats deadly fire followed. Capt. Agnnatuk was the first to figure it out. The Hellcats could somehow follow the repatriated officers even under the thick forest canopy.

"*Sisters, strip!*" she yelled tearing off her own clothes to set an immediate example. The officers quickly tore off their own clothes until they were running through the underbrush completely nude. Shortly they turned and looked back. The area where their clothes laid was being blasted by the Hellcats. It was their clothes that the Hellcats had zeroed in on.

A few moments later, at the forest edge a Hellcat lightly touched down. Overhead other Hellcats could be heard covering the area. The naked Miurruk officers crouched down behind any piece of bushy cover they could and watched and waited. They watched as two crew members came from the Hellcat, side arms drawn. The two crew members proceeded cautiously to the charred spot were most of their fire had been directed. All they found was destroyed clothing. One of the crew members, probably an officer, reached down and picked up a smoldering blouse. He looked around in the distance, even towards the women, trying to catch a clue as to where everyone might have gone. He saw no one. He threw the tattered blouse down and he and his other crew member headed back to their Hellcat. They climbed aboard and in a minute they were skyward bound.

As soon as the sound of Hellcats disappeared, the women came out from their hiding places. Adm. Enitir was the only officer dressed. "*Well*," she said as her young, naked officers gathered around her. "*Now we know to what trickery these bastards will stoop. Fortunately the battalions were dispersed and camped elsewhere.*" She looked at her XO. "*Good call, daughter. Okay, sisters, let's find you some uniforms.*" Amazingly no one had been killed, although several of the women required medical attention for superficial injuries.

"Sir? Col. Hicks is on hold for you."

Col. Eastman turned to the RTO, "Okay, I'll take it in my office." Bob Eastman had been expecting this call and he wanted it in private.

"Good Afternoon, John. How are you doing?"

"It's been better, Sir." The 1st Marine Brigade Commander paused. "Sir, I just had Lt Col. Carter and her S3 in my office and they expressed some concern about the consequences of the mission earlier this afternoon."

"Was Ben Errington upset?"

Hicks chuckled, "He was livid."

"He understands our need to locate the enemy, doesn't he?"

"Oh yes, Sir. He had no problems with that. It was the fact that we subsequently attacked them. Since we returned the PW's as a goodwill gesture, even told them so, and then turn around and attack them, he feels, well, he feels we slammed the door on any kind of peaceful reconciliation. He's afraid they'll never trust us now."

"Well, he may be right."

"I understand the BDA (Battle Damage Assessment) came back negative."

"Yeah, I think all we did was force them deeper into hiding, and we never found any line units," Eastman paused. "John, from the information Lilly Ng's people have gleaned out of the new PW's, they are less than brigade strength. There's no way they would attack us in force without reinforcements. I'm afraid they may go to unconventional warfare, especially after today's foray. I'm notifying all units."

"Yes, Sir. I'll alert the brigade."

Another month had passed with no enemy activity being reported anywhere. In fact the Miurruks were very active. They reorganized their battalions into light strike squads and prepared them for long range operations into enemy territory. Three battalion headquarters were established to control the missions of their assigned strike squads, to gather and disseminate information, and to act as a collection point for enemy prisoners.

Adm. Enitir also moved her headquarters closer and established a base for the final holding of prisoners and for the initiation of race regeneration. The new base was concealed in the Echo Mountain Range many kilometers south of Athenaburg. Tucked away in one of the numerous valleys, the new base camp was to become the hideaway city known to the Miurruks as Lanatuk and to the Herans as Pan. The only disadvantage to this location was the St. Ursula River stretched between Athenaburg and Lanatuk. Units are always vulnerable during river crossings.

Adm. Enitir didn't mind the wait. It ensured her that her people were ready, allowed time for the reinforcements to draw nearer, and hopefully was leading the invaders into a false sense of security. She picked a night when the moons were both near 100% illumination making the dark side of Malerdorn very bright. She instructed the battalions to have their strike squads attack shortly after midnight. This would be when pickets started falling asleep and give her strike squads plenty of time to regress. They were to get through the lines and hit a few of the farmers in the security zone west of Athenaburg towards the sea. They were to take as many prisoners as possible. They were not to engage the enemy unless fired upon and they were not to burn any structures for the fires would alarm others.

Getting past the 1st Divisions rookie pickets proved easy. A road had been constructed behind the perimeter to facilitate the movement of troops back and forth along the line of sentries. Once the squads crossed that road, they had pretty much left the armed contingent of the invaders behind. Two squads each went to different farmhouses. As this was the first mission, the Miurruks doubled teamed in case there were problems. There were no dogs or anything like that to worry about, but sophisticated alarm systems had been installed. The Miurruk warriors decided not to try and defeat the systems; instead they chose to overload the main system.

With watches synchronized, thirty squads broke into fifteen houses at precisely the same moment. Back at 1st Division Headquarters, the duty officer was alerted by the division monitoring station down the hall.

"Sir, I just got a whole bunch of alarms go off at once in the third and fifth sectors," the monitoring chief reported.

The duty officer rushed to the monitoring room. "Has anyone reported any trouble?"

"No, Sir."

The duty officer went back to his duty room where the duty sergeant was waiting. "Call all the brigades," he directed. "See if any have reported anything unusual and have them contact each post to be sure they're all right. Then have them call us back ASAP with their status."

The duty officer returned to monitoring room and paced back and forth until the status reports came in. When the duty sergeant informed the duty officer that all brigades reported nothing unusual, the duty officer picked up the phone and called the division G3.

"Sir, we've had a series of intrusion alarms go off in sectors three and five."

The G3 was still trying to wake up. "Has anyone reported anything?"

"No, Sir," the duty officer replied.

"Have you contacted the brigades?"

"Yes, Sir. They report no unusual incidents, Sir."

"Hmmm, probably just a fault in the system. We can check it out in the morning."

"Should I send a patrol around and makes sure everyone is okay?"

"And wake everyone up at this hour? I should say not. The community would be in an uproar. We'll check it in the morning, and Captain?"

"Yes, Sir?"

"Don't wake me up again unless somebody is shooting at somebody."

"Yes, Sir."

"What did the G3 say?"

The duty officer turned around to answer his duty sergeant. "They'll check it out in the morning and not to wake him up unless somebody is shooting at somebody."

"Sounds like a plan to me," the sergeant chuckled and then he turned and returned to his station in the duty office.

The warrior women broke into fifteen homes simultaneously and, with their weapons at the ready, stormed through each house rousing the startled settlers from their sleep. Allowing them to only throw on a jacket over their sleepwear and shoes on their feet, the Miurruks led the frighten settlers and any children they might have out into the warm Hera night. With both moons shining down to show the way, the alien women marched the terrified invader families down the paths toward the northern perimeter boundary. Forcing by threat of death to keep quiet, the Miurruks snuck the prisoners through the 1st Infantry Brigade lines and into the cover of the trees. Quietly, efficiently, they marched the prisoners to their respective battalion headquarters.

One outpost did report someone out to their front at one time. But when they answered the duty officer that no shots were fired, the incident was dismissed.

By midmorning the next day, all hell had broken loose at III Intergalactic Headquarters. The interim city mayor and his councilmen and women were fit to be tied.

The 1st Division Commander and the G3 were standing with their heels locked in the position of attention in LG. Eastman's office as the interim mayor, Sean O'Leary, ranted about the lack of professionalism that allowed forty-seven of his citizens to be kidnapped under the very noses of those chosen to protect.

Bob Eastman sat behind his desk and silently took volley after volley of accusations from the irate civilian. When O'Leary had spent himself out, Bob rose from his desk and apologized sincerely. He assured the interim mayor that all would be done to recover his citizens and then politely showed the mayor and his entourage the door.

LG. Eastman returned to his desk, picked up the duty officer's journal, and read over it one more time. When he got to the part about the incident, he read parts out loud; with each sentence his voice grew louder and angrier. "The G3 said it would be checked in the morning. Don't send out patrols as it would disturb the people. The G3 said he was not to be awoken unless shots were fired." Eastman threw the journal on his desk and pointed after the mayor. "He's right, you know. This is totally unprofessional." He glared at the commander and G3. The G3 lowered his eyes to the floor in shame.

"Sir, in light of this, I think it best if I tendered my resignation," the division commander said weakly.

"No, damn it. Denied," Eastman yelled as he threw the journal to the startled commander. "Get out there and do your jobs. Find those people." Eastman took a couple of breaths and turned his head away from the division commander and the G3. "Get out of my office," he said almost under his breath.

Patrols were sent out from all three of the 1st Divisions brigades and from the 1st Marine Brigade as well. No traces of the missing civilians were found, but the footprints in and out of the farmhouse areas were definitely those identified with Miurruk forces. All units were put on a heightened level of alert, but the forests and the meadows remained quiet.

The kidnapped civilians and their kidnappers had actually departed the area long before daybreak. The settlers were rushed to the battalion headquarters, shoved into shuttles and stealthfully whisked off to Lanatuk. The shuttles took long circuitous routes to avoid detection. The silent hovercraft moved quietly and quickly over the rough terrain, leaving no traces save some overturned leaves as they zipped just above the ground. They easily crossed the St. Ursula River far upstream from Athenaburg and her defensive forces and raced towards the Echo Mountains just as the sun was coming up in the east. By the time III Corps knew what hit them; the shuttles were half way to the mountains in the south.

Unfortunately for the hapless settlers, long range patrols and reconnaissance concentrated to the east; where the Miurruks had formerly camped. III Corps was totally unaware that Adm. Enitir had moved her camp to the Echo Mountains.

The Miurruks had been living off the land for some time now. Hera was teeming with large populations of animals suitable for the table as well as lush vegetation with a large variety of edible tubers, beans, grains and leaves. They immediately recognized the invaders' interest in this planet and decided it ideal for their own habitation.

Neither were the women wasteful or without knowledge of the wilderness. They had a memory, from where they did not know, but definitely not Miurruk, that reminded them how to use plants, animals, and the very dirt beneath their feet to their advantage. Unbeknownst to everyone but the fathers, the Miurruk women were special among their species, special among the universe. That fraction of one percent in their unique genetic pool gave them a power not even the women of Miurruk had yet fully appreciated. It was the power of magic; not to turn a prince into a frog, but to know and understand things past, long past.

They could touch a man's scar and know what inflicted the pain. They could touch a plant and remember from their forebears eons ago on an earth so far away how to use that type of plant even though it was different from those their forebears used. They could gently lay their fingers in a sign or track of an animal and know the animal and follow it readily. They were learning to read the sky, and the rivers, and the mountains themselves. Detached from their closed-in urban existence as servants on Miurruk, the women of Miurruk were being reborn. They could never return now. They were becoming more akin to Malerdorn than even their invader cousins could ever know or be.

So the women used their untapped gifts and learned ever so quickly how to not only survive, but how to prosper on this new planet. They saved the skins of the animals they harvested for their meat to fashion into clothing to replace the tattering uniforms that thinned and weakened in time and use. In the mountains they found animals with hair and made clothing and wrappings to stave off the cold breath of the Echo Mountains. They lived well, they ate well, and they even drank well from mead and beer they had learned to make. As memories of Miurruk faded in the past, the Miurruk women were becoming one with Malerdorn. They were no longer Miurruk; they were Malerdorns.

On the other hand, their invader cousins, the prisoners, puzzled them. They possessed neither the natural gifts nor the love of Malerdorn that the Malerdorns had. They called the planet Hera and themselves Herans and a broad division of misunderstanding and distrust rifted between them. They knew neither the plants nor the animals that fed and clothe them, they could read nothing but books, and the mountain had no sympathy for them. It cut their feet, made them sick, and chilled their flesh with its bitter bite.

Fortunately the Malerdorns were for the most part good to them. Their enslavement was not as physically harsh as it was morally unacceptable. The Malerdorns needed the Herans for one main reason; to increase their numbers, which meant breeding. Unlike the traditional means of artificial insemination, the Malerdorns were learning sex with males. The Malerdorn women found this new method of fertilization most agreeable and were very eager to adopt it into their culture. Unfortunately the fifteen households from which the settlers were taken were all married couples, and the Heran women were quite resentful of their Malerdorn captors using their mates no matter how good the cause. More prisoners needed to be taken.

The next raid on the Athenaburg invaders was on the next Ares full moon; Hebe was on the other side of the planet. This time the Malerdorn women were more selective. They understood the orders of Adm. Enitir, who was most interested in getting the invaders out, but the Malerdorns were more interested in mates. A slight variation of orders couldn't hurt, and since Enitir never left Lanatuk, she would never be the wiser.

This time they hit the 2nd Brigade, 1st ID sector along the St. Ursula River. Again they waited until late in the evening when the weeks' long lack of activity and the late night hours pushed the Heran pickets to their alertness limit. The Malerdorns silently overtook the first position; two women. This would never do. They securely bound them and left a couple of guards. They knew their time was limited because the Herans' headquarters would surely be making periodic commo checks.

Half of the strike squads went east and the other half, west. Up and down the line they came across drowsy pickets, some male and some female, but mostly male. They brought them all back to the initial location and bounded the females together. With this sector of the perimeter in Malerdorn hands, they brought the shuttles skimming across the waters of the St. Ursula and loaded the men onboard. The Malerdorns climbed aboard as one Malerdorn woman took out a marker and wrote a couple of letters on each Heran woman's forehead. Then she too hopped into a shuttle and they headed down the embankment and out over the water into the darkness.

Unanswered commo checks from the 2nd Brigade Headquarters sent the brigade ready reaction force scurrying out to the perimeter. Empty position upon empty position was not a good sign and with each report the brigade commander and the division commander, both of whom were subsequently awaken and now at their respective headquarters, were becoming increasingly concerned. A bit of relief came when the women soldiers were found all tied together, but alive and well. However, nineteen male soldiers were missing.

There was no doubt this time as to what had happened. LG Eastman just buried his face in his hands as the report was read to him. He wanted to fire the lot, but what good would that do? But when he heard the portion about the scribbling on the female soldiers' foreheads, his ears perked up. According to translation from one of the Miurruk translators, the message read to the effect, 'You can keep your sluts.'

Bob Eastman lifted his head from his hands. "Say again," he said cocking his head forward and to one side. When it was repeated, he leaned back in his chair, sat silently for a moment, and said, "Get me Major Errington here; now."

As Ben Errington listened to the reports and the message written on the 1st Division soldiers' foreheads, he stared blankly at the floor.

"What do you make of it, Ben?" the Corps commander asked.

Ben sat quietly for a moment biting his lower lip. He tried to put it all together; since day one. "Sir," he said finally. "The Miurruks attacked the 14th when it first arrived. I believe that the Miurruks had no idea who they were attacking. After they found out, they attacked again; that time prepared to take specimens and prisoners, something they did not do the first time. Also during those attacks they took no women.

Then they raided the settlements and took entire families; husbands, wives, and children. But this last raid, they took only men, leaving the women behind with this message about us keeping the women.

"Sir, except for my wife, the raid on the settlement was the first time they took female prisons."

"How is your wife?" Bob asked genuinely concerned.

"She's doing well, thank you, Sir. During her convalescence and even now she has been working with the crossovers. She is learning their language and gained their confidence. I believe she has gained a lot of insight into their psyche and culture. Did you know that the Miurruk women can touch a scar on a complete stranger and understand how the scar was brought on?"

"No, I didn't know that."

"Sir, I can't answer for their leaders, but I believe the Miurruks are basically good women. Even the doctor that took our baby struggled to untie Nina from the gurney with gunfire from the Hellcats raining down around her. Even with me pointing a gun to her head, she freed Nina before she fled. This is not the action of a murderess or a terrorist. I believe the Miurruks need us to regenerate their race. They have never summarily executed anyone to our knowledge. Prisoners they have not taken, they have left behind unharmed. They took our women one time. Apparently that failed. So the next time they took just men and left a message describing their dissatisfaction with the previous experience. Sir, I really believe we should talk to Nina."

Bob Eastman touched a window on his flush, desktop computer screen.

"Yes, Sir?" came the reply.

"John," Bob said to his clerk. "Would you please send in Turrigan?"

"Yes, Sir."

A moment later, Turrigan, a III Corps Miurruk translator came in. Bob unbuttoned the top two buttons to his uniform blouse, and pulled the collar to one side exposing a four centimeter long scar on his collarbone. "Turrigan, touch this."

Turrigan hesitated then slowly reached forward placing her first three fingers on the General's scar. Shortly her face grew red and she giggled an uneasy, embarrassed laugh. "Sir, you should be ashamed."

"Okay, Turrigan, that's all for now."

"When I was a fresh lieutenant," LG. Eastman explained as he buttoned up his shirt. "I got in a bar fight over some bar girl. A broken beer bottle caused this."

Ben smiled. Eastman again called his clerk. "John, please send for Cpt. Nina Errington at 1st Brigade Corps."

"Right away, Sir."

"Not a word about the scar to anyone, Errington," Eastman smirked.

"No, Sir," Ben smiled. "Not a word; to anyone."

CHAPTER ELEVEN

Nina reported to LG. Eastman's office as instructed. Since her convalescence she had been working as the Assistant S3 (Operations) on the brigade staff at 1st Marine Brigade Headquarters. She didn't mind the work, but she missed the responsibility of command and wished she had her company back.

She, LG Eastman, and Ben discussed the situation concerning the Miurruk kidnappings. The Miurruk warrior women were proving to be more than III Corps could handle given its current resources. They were moving in and out of the security area too easily and had been responsible for the taking of sixty-six men, women, and children to date. The civilian settlers were scared and were losing confidence in C.O.P.E.'s and their own security force's ability to protect them. Eastman needed to somehow turn this situation around.

"Do you think the crossovers would help us?" he asked hopefully.

"Help us how?" Nina asked.

"I don't know; as scouts or something like that. Our history is full of examples where an army has used people from the same culture as its enemy to help it fight the enemy."

"I don't know, they might if I ask them to," Nina shrugged.

"I want you to find out if they will," Bob Eastman directed. "They are of the same race; maybe the crossovers understand the Miurruk and can help us head them off before they strike again."

"You don't think they'll object to betraying their own people?" Ben asked.

"I've learned that the Miurruk women are good people," Nina replied. "The crossovers generally don't agree with the policies of Miurruk and don't accept this war. That's why they crossed over. Maybe, just maybe, if I explain that they can help us stop the hostilities and bring peace to the planet, then they will help us."

"Good," Eastman said slapping his hands on his desk. "I'm going to form a new unit, Nina; a company of Miurruk scouts, and I want to put you in command." Eastman stood up and paced in front of his desk as he thought out loud. "It will be assigned to 1st Marine Brigade for support but will receive its taskings from III Corps, G3. You will report directly to Colonel Steinfeld. Your Miurruks will accompany unit patrols from 1st Division and 1st Marine Brigade. They will assist the patrol leaders in finding the enemy and/or avoiding possible trouble spots. You will recruit them, train them, and coordinate their link-ups with the other units." He looked at Nina. "Do you think they'll wear our uniforms?"

"I don't know, Sir," she replied shaking her head.

Eastman shrugged, "If not we'll make them their own, but I want them out of the Miurruk uniforms; I want them to understand that they now give their allegiance to us."

"Yes, Sir."

"Any questions?"

"Will they be paid, Sir?"

"Yes. They'll receive the same benefits as any C.O.P.E. soldier," Eastman said as he mulled over the requirements to get that passed through the bureaucracy. "If they're willing to wear the C.O.P.E. uniform, then we can just enlist them. That will smooth the paper chase and get them their benefits immediately. Tell them that; that might help recruitment.

"Any other questions?"

"No, Sir," Nina smiled as she and Ben stood up to leave.

"Good," Eastman smiled. "I'll have G1 (Personnel) cut the orders today."

Ben and Nina departed III Corps Headquarters and rode back to brigade in the same CATV. En route they stopped and had lunch at one of the newly established eateries. They ate out on the terrace and watched the people parade by going about their daily business. The air was clean, although a little humid. There were none of the big city noises that Ben and Nina were used to back on earth. Everything was relatively quiet under a warm blue Hera sky. They lightly held hands as they chatted. They talked of distant dreams and safer times. They allowed the love they had between them to glow in the bright Heran sunshine. Ben and Nina seldom had moments like this anymore. They were caught up in the first war in the Race's recent history and with the tactics now being employed by the Miurruks, there was no end in sight.

True to his word, LG. Eastman had the orders cut that afternoon and the following day, Cpt. Nina Errington was out recruiting scouts. She went first to the crossovers who had touched her scar. She figured she would have the most luck with them. Nina explained why she needed their help and told them what sort of rewards in the way of benefits and even citizenship they could enjoy. She put the best face on it she could. At first the women were hesitant, not so much because of loyalty to the fathers as fear of retribution. Finally one girl, Ngnanatuk, said she would help and that opened the door for the others. Nina was able to get about a dozen women from that group.

She put them into C.O.P.E. military uniforms as soon as she could so they would immediately feel like part of the Race and no longer part of the Miurruk world. And Nina had to give the company a name. She wanted something that the women would readily adopt and that was not Miurruk. Nina thought the best way to do that was to put it to the women, and if the name was acceptable, they would surely stand proudly by it. They batted around several names, trying each one on like a new dress. First of all they were all women, so some thought the name should have the word 'women' in it. Secondly, they were going to be scouts so the name should have something to do with scouts, reconnaissance, or something similar in it. And finally, since it was a unique unit, the name should reflect that as well. They finally decided on Women's Reconnaissance Patrol or WRPs (pronounced werps) for short.

As soon as she got the first group into uniforms, she took them out with her to recruit other members for the company. Cpt. Errington was able to recruit thirty-seven Miurruk women the first week. The second week; training began.

With the help of the brigade training NCO, Nina set up a training program that would run the woman through a mini-basics course as well as the art of scouting. They would be trained on the M12P as their basic individual weapon. They would learn map reading, navigation, equipment recognition, survival, first aid, and a host of other subjects to prepare them for a hostile field environment. In addition to all that, they would have to learn military courtesy and customs and a continuation of English conversation peppered with military acronyms. She had a lot to train them on and she only had six weeks. Fortunately, the Miurruk women were quick learners with exceptional memory skills.

The women were billeted in new barracks inside the brigade compound. They dressed like marines, talked like marines, and soon walked like marines. They were immediately accepted by their Race counterparts and the distinction between Race and Miurruk soon faded. The women enjoyed a sense of equality and acceptance they had never known before and their allegiance grew rock solid. The WRPs trained hard and were eager to learn. They adopted military custom and courtesy not so much because they had to, but because they wanted to. Nina received several compliments on the WRPs military bearing and courtesy and this made her very proud. When the sixth week came, Cpt. Errington knew she and her girls were ready and she over boiled with excitement.

After the sixth week was completed, III Intergalactic Corps held a Unit Commissioning Ceremony for the Women's Reconnaissance Patrol, Hera to inaugurate the unit officially into the C.O.P.E. Armed Forces. As a separate and independent unit, the unit was presented its official unit colors, unit crest, and shoulder patch. A few of the WRP's were also promoted initiating a command structure in the company. The formal ceremony was presided over by LG. Eastman, with all division, brigade, and battalion commanders present. The local citizenry was invited and the other crossovers were required to attend. The parade formation included the 1st Marine Brigade commander and staff and the commander and staff and one company from each of its three battalions and the WRP Company. The other companies remained on the perimeter.

It was the first official ceremony on Hera. Bob Eastman also recognized this as an opportunity for the military to present itself in a favorable light to the anxious civilian community, so there were vehicles and equipment displays as well as a partially restored boomerang fighter. There were refreshment stands and III Corps sponsored a barbecue that would have made even the most homesick settler feel at home. But most importantly, when the crossovers watched the proud WRPs pass smartly in review in the ceremony and saw the warmest of welcomes they received from the Herans, recruitment tripled the following week. Cpt. Errington had her company.

Through coordination with Corps G3, Nina tasked her WRPs to accompany certain patrols from the 1st Division and the 1st Marine Brigade. She was very busy in the initial weeks as she had to balance training of the new recruits with mission requirements. When time permitted, she would accompany a patrol to check the effectiveness and interaction of her WRPs with the members of the unit patrol. After every patrol, Nina would have her WRP team debrief in front of the entire company so everyone could learn from the team's experience, from its good points, and where it made mistakes.

The long hours of WRP's training finally paid off in the second month. One of the WRP teams out on patrol with a squad from Bravo Company, 3rd Battalion, 1st Brigade, 1st Infantry Division read the signs now familiar to them. An alien patrol was coming. The two women alerted the patrol leader who immediately set up a hasty ambush. As the enemy patrol wandered into the firetrap one of the WRPs called out in Miurruk.

"Sisters, stop. Drop your weapons or we will be forced to kill you."

But the Malerdorn patrol leader was one of the hard core loyalists and she refused to surrender lightly. She fired bursts into the brush around the general direction from which the WRP's voice came. Her shots were answered by a hailstorm of bright red M12P fire from the Bravo Company squad in an exchange that lasted less than ten seconds. In the end seven alien soldiers lay dead, two were seriously wounded and one just too afraid to stick her head up.

The two wounded were medevacked to the 14th's FAV along with the unharmed prisoner who had military police and an interrogation team waiting for her. The squad wanted to recover the dead, but the WRPs were adamantly opposed. They insisted on taking their weapons and equipment, but the bodies should be left behind. When asked why, the WRPs said that the enemy would find them and lay hands on their wounds and know what had happened here. It would serve as a warning. With sisters, they don't need to use markers on foreheads, one of the WRPs pointed out.

News of the ambush whipped through Athenaburg and the military community like a rocket. New hope was raised against their chances in this sordid type of warfare, and more importantly, trust with their new found sisters from a distant planet solidified. Not only did the citizens trust the crossovers more, but the soldiers who went out on patrol with them grew to trust and respect them.

That afternoon Cpt. Errington, Col. Steinfeld, Col. Ng, and Maj. Southerland met in LG. Eastman's office. Much had been learned through their new prisoners especially the young woman who kept her head buried.

"For one thing," Lilly Ng started off. "Their headquarters no longer lies in the west. They've moved it somewhere in the Echo Mountains. The prisoners say they are not sure where; they claim they've never been there.

"Apparently they have three field headquarters. Judging from the size of this patrol's headquarters, assuming that their sizes are similar, the headquarters are about battalion strength which means they may have a brigade equivalency in the field."

"That's not so much," Southerland interjected.

Ng looked at him through the corner of her eyes and continued. "Using this type of unconventional warfare, a company of insurgents in the field can easily tie up a brigade which means they have more than enough troops in the field to keep us on the defensive with the resources we have on the ground." LG. Eastman shifted uncomfortably in his chair.

"On a more significant note; one I'm sure Nina can attest to, they no longer refer to themselves as Miurruks. They have renamed themselves Malerdorns. We have known for sometime that the Miurruk name for Hera is Malerdorn. The fact that they have converted their identity to this planet means they are here for the long haul. They do not plan to leave."

Bob Eastman sat erect in his chair. "Nina?"

"Yes, Sir," she concurred. "My girls confirm it. Their leader, one Admiral Enitir," Nina looked at Lilly who nodded approval of Nina taking the ball, "has apparently decided to break away from a slave-like existence on Miurruk and start a new life for her sisters; that is to say her people, here. From what we've learned, she plans to take over Hera as her own and then go free the rest of her sisters from the cruel hands of their alien masters. Apparently, Sir, these are real aliens; nothing like us."

Eastman raised his hands slightly. "Can't we share this planet?"

"As we understand, some of the Miurruks, or Malerdorns, know the history of earth, or at least parts of it. Admiral Enitir is one of them. Because of our aggressive, warlike past, she has no trust in us. Perhaps we could have argued sharing the planet when we released their prisoners," Nina said cautiously. "But after we attacked them…."

Eastman waved off the rest with a violent motion of his left hand, and then he stood up. "Damn it, people. We've got the next wave of immigrants arriving the next quarter. And as we all know, 5th Frontier Fleet Command is also in that convoy. They are not going to be happy to learn that a group of insurgents only about two thousand strong are holding up the settlement of almost one hundred thousand people."

"There's one other thing we found out," Ng interjected.

Eastman threw up his hands. "Oh, please," he said awaiting the bad news.

"They're using shuttles to move soldiers and prisoners around. Well, these shuttles are hovercraft. We've apparently have only seen them in the 'wheels-down' configuration. That was probably by designed," Lilly nodded. "We always thought that they were using different modes of transportation to get people back and forth to the other end of the planet. But apparently these shuttles move like a jet doing NOE (Knap of Earth)."

"So our estimates as to where their camps may be considering movement by foot or ground vehicle may be totally erroneous?" Eastman asked.

"I'm afraid so, Sir."

"Heinrich," Eastman said diverting his attention to his G3. "I haven't heard a thing from you today."

"Sir, we can increase our patrols and send out reconnaissance to the south and in the Echo Mountains, but unless we can knock Admiral Enitir and her cadre out…"

"That's like peeing on a forest fire, Heinrich."

"Which brings me to a suggestion, Sir."

"Tell me, Nina," Eastman said.

"My WRPs are pretty sure they can find their mountain hideout."

"Nina, the Echo Mountain Range is as large as the Rocky Mountains. How is a company going to find anyone in an area so vast and rugged?" Eastman asked.

"My girls are pretty sure Enitir is not hiking the prisoners in so she has to be using the hovercraft. These hovercrafts have physical limitations in both the hover and wheels-down mode. They cannot go up very steep inclines, over any obstacle over one meter high, or through densely wooded areas. My girls are also sure that Enitir is somewhere near the closest part of the range due to fuel limitations and so as not to expose the hovercraft to possible observation too long, even in the stealth mode. Through detailed satellite imagery indicating slope, dense vegetation, and objects down to one meter in size, they believe they can at least narrow down the search field to a manageable size."

Eastman looked over at Lilly. "It's feasible, Sir," she nodded. "By narrowing down the number of tracts they can use will save us a lot of time and effort." Ng shrugged, "The imagery is simple. And if we keep a bird in geosynchronous orbit, patch down the imagery right here to Corps HQ, we should be able to have a good footprint of the area in a day or so."

"Geosynchronous orbit is pretty high up, Lilly. Can we get detailed pictures from there?" Eastman cocked his head to one side and squinted.

"Oh, yes, Sir," Ng winked an assurance. "Even in cloudy weather."

Bob Eastman rubbed his chin. 5th Frontier Fleet would be here in the next quarter with a new batch of settlers. It would be great if this conflict were resolved by the time they arrived. "Okay," he said slapping his palms on the desk. "Let's get the imagery, find the footprint, and send a task force to clean them out."

"Sir," Nina said as she stepped forward. "With all due respect, my girls want this shot."

"Nina, I appreciate their willingness to help, but this is a job for a combat unit."

"Sir, they are a combat unit. I trained them," she defended.

"Nina, I understand that they did not return fire on the Malerdorn patrol earlier. I want people who can fight."

"Sir, if I may explain," Nina paused as the Corps Commander sat back down in his chair. True to the mark of a good commander, Eastman listened to his people. "What happened this morning was an anomaly. When my WRPs advised the Malerdorn patrol to surrender, they expected it to happen. They thought their sisters would surrender and then call my girls traitors or something like that. This thought has occurred to my girls for quite some time.

"However the Malerdorn patrol leader did not surrender. She shot at my WRPs with the intent to kill. The girls were dumbstruck. They never expected a sister to fire on them. The firefight lasted only seconds; they never had a chance to recover from their initial shock and return fire. When they returned from the mission, the barracks was ablaze with talk of the incident. Enitir and her loyalists are now truly considered the enemy. The Malerdorn patrol leader sealed it. I guarantee, Sir. The next time, deadly fire will be returned by my WRPs.

"Sir, there is still a brigade-size enemy unit out there somewhere. We need our combat units here to protect Athenaburg. Let me and my girls do it, Sir. Give us a shot."

Eastman leaned back in his chair and thought for a moment. "Let me sleep on it," he finally said. "Lilly, get me those images. Heinrich, continue the patrols with the WRPs attached. Questions? Okay, everyone, that's all for now. Back to work."

Over the next few days the satellite was positioned above the northwest corner of the Echo Mountains and imagery detailing the slope down to a one meter resolution started pouring in. LG. Eastman slept on the request from Cpt. Errington but was still not prepared to send in the infant reconnaissance company on its own, especially since, except for Nina, the entire unit was made up of crossovers. Instead Bob Eastman directed the 1st Marine Brigade to send in its 1st Battalion with the WRP Company, minus one platoon, attached. The WRP platoon left behind would continue to support the 1st Infantry Division and the remainder of the 1st Marine Brigade protecting Athenaburg.

Eastman watched with interest as handfuls of WRPs filed into the G2 section every morning and every evening to pour over the satellite imagery. Even though their English was by then considered at the advanced level, they would chatter away in their native Miurruk like a bunch of schoolgirls. It gave the commander and staff a rare opportunity to listen to Miurruk conversation and helped the people of the earth put a voice to the women's culture, to their race, and to the enemy. It gave the Race a rare insight to their children lost so many centuries ago.

However the WRPs industry was professional. Using different color markers, the WRPs outlined different grades of slope and one meter plus sized objects. They started with the flattest areas and color coded them green. Difficult or questionable slope they painted yellow and impossible slope and dense wooded areas were delegated red. Soon discernable tracts became readily apparent and a footprint of negotiable terrain of the mountainous area emerged. Surprisingly, despite the large area of the northeast corner of the Echo Mountains that was imaged, only twelve tracts were deemed suitable for sustained operations. Two of those tracts emerged as passages to the other side of the mountains; valuable information for future Hera development.

In the meantime, Lt Col. Carter was preparing her battalion to deploy south to the foothills of the Echo Mountains. There she would establish her TOC and set up her battalion for sustained mountain operations. Maj. Errington found himself the busiest he had ever been in his life; selecting routes of movement and march orders for the companies including the WRP Company (minus); meaning minus one platoon, selecting three or four areas that appeared suitable for the battalion's deployment, and developing the Operations Order for battalion and WRP Company operations.

The Malerdorns were not sitting on their haunches during this time. The loss of their one patrol in such a dastardly ambush that included treacherous sisters infuriated the Admiral and she increased attacks on the invaders. These attacks included ambushing a supply convoy which left several dead 1st Infantry Division soldiers as well as several new captives for the Malerdorns.

In that incident two squads of Malerdorn warriors slipped through the 3rd Battalions lines near the coast and set up an ambush along the perimeter road. They hid themselves in the wood line with one squad laying in wait parallel to the road, the other perpendicular to the road with half the squad on each side of the thoroughfare. This effected a classic 'L' ambush.

The convoy came rumbling down the road; a CATV front and rear and six cargo movers, or CMPVs. The Malerdorns waited until the convoy was well within the ambush kill zone and simultaneously opened fire. The squad perpendicular to the road hit the convoy broadside, every vehicle struck by yellow darts of searing death at once. The squad paralleling the road fired down both sides of the road striking down anyone leaving the vehicles. The effective ambush lasted less than twenty seconds, leaving a dozen dead and wounded soldiers on the road and five prisoners.

The Malerdorns couldn't transport the wounded so they applied immediate first aid, ensuring that any profuse bleeding had been stopped and all were breathing on their own. The women collected the prisoners and quickly left the dead and wounded and a line of burning vehicles on the road even as a ready reaction platoon could be heard approaching in the distance.

Up and down the perimeter the Malerdorns were enjoying much success with their hit and run tactics. A prisoner here and a prisoner there kept the shuttles busy in their runs back and forth to the Echo Mountains hideout, Lanatuk. The Herans were growing more and more disconcerted everyday.

Patrols were increased and several times fire fights ensued. True to Nina's word the WRPs returned fire with deadly accuracy as they watched sister upon sister die in a hail of red darts of concentrated radiation. Both sides were losing what they considered unacceptable losses, but this only served to strengthen each side's resolve.

Finally after two weeks of preparation the 1st Marine Battalion and WRP Company (minus) moved out. They moved to the St. Ursula River, secured both sides and then crossed it with their swim-capable CMPVs. Lt Col. Glenda Carter wasn't taking any chances. The last thing she wanted was to be caught of guard in a deadly ambush. She continuously scouted ahead and along the flanks with Cpt. Errington's WRPs in CATVs.

They crossed the floodplain with its low-lying meadows punctuated with bogs and marshes teeming with wildlife until they reached the Southbend River. They crossed the river and made camp on its high northern banks. Progress so far had been good with no sign of enemy forces.

But their approach had not gone unnoticed. Malerdorn patrols on the southern side of the rivers watched from a distance as the large convoys headed south. Admiral Enitir was informed of the large troop movements towards her. She determined that the invaders were closing on her to seek her out. Surely if they knew her location, they would have sent in their Hellcats and attacked en masse. She pulled in her southern battalion to set up defenses along the approaches. Her other two battalions in the field would have to continue the guerilla operations against Athenaburg alone.

By the end of the second day, Lt Col. Carter's battalion had moved into the high plains approaching the rolling foothills of the mountains. Their journey, now at the halfway mark, would proceed much faster since they had left the rivers and boggy lowlands behind. In open terrain such as this, the 4th Tank Battalions tanks would be useful; but where she was leading her units was not tank country, so no tanks were brought.

The battalion moved more quickly over the high plains with its shimmering grain grasses undulating in the breezes. Off in the distance, large herds of meadow grazers could be seen enjoying some of the many fruits of the planet.

By the end of the third day, the 1st Marine Battalion had moved into the foothills where trees began popping up more numerously. Soon they would be in the wooded foothills that butted up tightly against the Echo Mountains, and there they would set up camp for continued operations.

On the fourth day they set up camp on some high ground overlooking the plains from whence they had come. It was good defendable terrain that afforded good visibility and fields of fire. The TOC was erected and the battalions dug in at their assigned locations with the WRP Company (minus) within the perimeter. Operations would begin immediately the following day. Reconnaissance patrols in force would start scouring the approaches into the mountain chain to find and root out Enitir and her warriors.

CHAPTER TWELVE

It was the first good news Adm. Enitir had received in ages, reinforcements had arrived. A division of infantry came in on a convoy of transports including more boomerang fighter aircraft. It would be the final reinforcements warned the fathers, all other troops and supply would remain on Miurruk to defend the planet.

Now the middle-aged admiral had some decisions to make. She could commit the forces here on Hera in hopes of eliminating the formidable invaders or she could use these fresh, but untried soldiers to fight the fathers for the release of the remainder of her race. The remainder would remain on Miurruk to fend off attacks from the invaders, the fathers said. But how many sisters did that include back on Miurruk, and would they fight her and her Malerdorns if she were to return to liberate the planet? Finally, how loyal were the new troops to Miurruk? Would they fight along side her in her quest to release the power of the fathers over the other sisters or would they deem that treason and defend Miurruk? Or worse yet, would there be crossovers among them when they learned of the situation here. Adm. Enitir decided to postpone deploying the new troops to Malerdorn just yet. First she must talk to the division commander. She wondered who that might be.

The division commander turned out to be another classmate of the admirals. Gen. Rotukana was a tall, handsome woman with long jet-black hair tied in a bun and turquoise eyes that shone like the clear Malerdorn sky. A fine figure of a woman, Rotukana always dominated any room she entered with her dignity and grace.

Enitir first met privately with Rotukana in her headquarters tucked in the mountains. The two old friends exchanged pleasantries and then sat down with a cup of tea from leaves picked in the cool Echo mountain air along the jagged slopes that concealed Lanatuk. The admiral's friend had brought grave news and she spoke frankly with Enitir.

"*The fathers are not encouraged by your progress here, Enitir. They have directed that you return to your duties at the fleet and that I take over the ground operations.*" Gen. Rotukana handed her the slate with the fathers' orders on it.

Enitir sat back in her chair and read the orders; this was not the news she wanted to hear. Even though she wanted to break away from Miurruk; she wanted to have control of the forces in Malerdorn so her plans could be realized. She would have no say on Malerdorn while she was in space with the fleet.

"*Scuttlebutt aboard the fleet is you have other designs, sister,*" Rotukana continued coolly and calmly as though she were discussing the weather. "*I've heard talk of liberation and independence and the words 'treason' and 'sedition' float on the wind. There was much excitement aboard the fleet during my passage over; dangerous excitement. Our spacefaring sisters, your daughters, now call themselves Malerdorns; Malerdorns on Miurruk vessels! And even now this talk is poisoning my troops with drunken illusions of freedom from tyranny. Tell me, sister; what shall I report to the fathers?*"

Enitir looked into Rotukana's big, beautiful turquoise eyes and tried to read her feelings, but she could discern nothing. "*It is not scuttlebutt, sister,*" Enitir finally said. "*It is in fact my plan to make Malerdorn the new home for us so we no longer must live under slavery.*" Enitir stood up and went to the map of Malerdorn and placed her hand on it. "*This world has everything we need. This world is good for us. You should see it, sister,*" she said, excitement raising her voice. "*Our sisters thrive off this land. Memories; long forgotten memories have returned to us here. Sisters pick up a leaf or a root and they remember how such things can be used and which are good for us and which are bad. We can read a river and know where the fish lie or where the water is sweet or where the crossing is easy. We can read the sky and know how to dress for the day."* She walked over and sat beside Rotukana and held her hands tightly. *"Join me, sister; join us,"* Enitir pleaded. Rotukana said nothing.

"I'm just an old spacedog," the admiral chuckled almost nervously with a sly, sweet pout. *"I'm not a land commander. Even now the invaders are in the foothills seeking us out. I am at wit's end on how to rout them. Be my general on the ground. Join us."*

"What happened to General Itunguh? Why isn't she leading her soldiers?"

"She never made Malerdorn," Enitir said as she lowered her head. *"Her transport was destroyed along with both of my carriers the first day. We lost many good sisters that day. And then we've lost many here. Why, some have even gone over to the invaders and helped these pirates,"* Enitir said indignantly. *"There is even a unit of sisters with this force in the foothills trying to discover Lanatuk,"* she cried pointing outside.

"Sisters have joined the other side?" Rotukana was shocked.

"Yes!" Enitir shouted.

"Why?"

"Some have lost the mettle to fight, if they ever had it. Some have become smitten with the male invaders." Enitir sighed heavily. *"Many of my own sisters have nestled with prisoners and then want to possess them. Then they become pregnant and lose their will to fight."* Enitir flopped back in her chair, her wrists resting on the chair's arms, and her chin on her chest in complete capitulation.

"I wanted the sisters to become pregnant," she confessed, *"to increase our numbers, but this method of lying with men has destroyed them. I mean artificial methods leave none of the emotional baggage*

my sisters are going through now. They've become possessive, jealous, conniving; I tell you, sister," she huffed. "*I've a good mind to ban all this sexual cavorting and require that only artificial methods be used.*"

"*Why don't you?*"

"*To be honest,*" the admiral resigned. "*I'm afraid I will lose them over to the invaders.*" Enitir looked away as though trying to stare out into the distance. "*I don't know what they see in lying with men.*"

"*You mean you haven't tried it?*"

"*Absolutely not!*" Enitir shot her head up indignantly.

"*Maybe you'd learn what all the hubbub's about,*" Rotukana defended.

"*And have myself acting like a foolish little schoolgirl?*"

"*At least you'd know what your sisters are going through.*"

"*It sounds to me like they're all going crazy.*"

"*It sounds to me like they are falling in love,*" Rotukana scoffed.

Adm. Enitir paused momentarily. "*Rotukana; sister; will you help me?*"

Gen. Rotukana smiled, "*Of course I will.*"

In the 1st Marine TOC Lt Col. Carter, Maj. Errington, and Cpt. Errington were huddled around the map. Lt Col. Carter wanted to increase the patrols which meant thinning out her perimeter security. She would leave one company behind to 'mind the fort' while the other two would send out platoon-size patrols. This would require tightening the perimeter around the battalion headquarters and bringing the company headquarters closer to the TOC, but she was counting on finding the enemy quicker by adding more patrols to the field. Cpt Errington requested and was granted permission to accompany one of the patrols. Glenda told her to hook up with Cpt. Montgomery down at Alpha Company.

Dawn the next morning, Nina and three of her WRPs were motoring out with 3rd Platoon, Alpha Company to reconnoiter one of the promising passes through the mountains. Helicopters would have been ideal, but except for the medevac and heavy-lift copters found in the 14th Terrestrial Division, none had been brought. The patrols found themselves doing it the old fashion way, by wheel and foot.

Nina and one of her WRPs were riding in the lead CATV with the platoon leader, Lt. Charlie Wiggins, while her other two WRPs were each in one of the two trailing CMPVs. As they bounced over the virgin terrain, Nina and Charlie checked and rechecked their positioning. With satellite down link, navigation was relatively simple and in little time they were driving southwest into the valley that formed the approach they were to scout.

The vehicles had been fitted with special skirts to give added protection against enemy small arms fire and all rode with their tops down to give the marines more visibility and so they could easily return fire if they were fired on. They traveled now in a vee formation with the CATV in the front center and the two CMPVs trailing out to the sides to better cover the narrow valley floor.

They had driven about thirty minutes up the valley when the WRP in the CATV asked Nina to stop the vehicle. The WRP, Ngnanatuk, jumped out of the vehicle and looked carefully around her. The other vehicles stopped as well and she was soon joined by her two WRP comrades, Sipatuk and Kanapang. Nina listened intently as the three girls chattered on in their native Miurruk. She could tell by their voices that they were growing increasingly concerned as they looked around them. Cpt. Errington was confident in her girls' abilities to read the

Malerdorns, so she directed Lt. Wiggins to radio the possibility of contact into his company.

Suddenly the girls dropped down and yelled in Miurruk to Nina, "*Mother, get down!*"

Nina yelled, "Out of the vehicle!" as she vaulted out of the CATV pivoting on one hand and landing beside the young women. Charlie and the driver cleared the CATV just as the first few yellow bolts stuck the interior of the vehicle sending sparks and bits of cushions into the air.

Up ahead on both sides of the valley Malerdorn soldiers opened up with a fury of small arms fire. Because they sensed the presence of their Malerdorn sisters, the WRPs had stopped the patrol before it had driven up into the kill zone of the ambush. The Malerdorns had fired prematurely because they sensed they had been spotted. This hasty action saved the platoon from annihilation.

Because the platoon had yet entered the kill zone, they were able to quickly dismount and deploy up the flank of both lines of Malerdorn soldiers on each side of the valley. They advanced cautiously but quickly along the boulders and trees that lined the valley walls. The Malerdorns, unsure what to do continued to fire on the six trapped by the burning CATV.

The three WRPs crawled between Nina and the Malerdorn positions and from the prone position quickly returned fire. Nina called in a quick SITREP (situation report) to battalion headquarters while Charlie and the driver also returned fire. The situation was not looking good as the yellow, energized darts splashed around them, sending dirt and grass into the air. Nina started to crawl backwards to get behind the burning CATV to try and put a little bit of metal between them and the Malerdorn positions. She grabbed the boot of one of her WRPs and shouted, "*Daughters, crawl back with me*;" and then to the platoon leader, "Charlie, pull back, pull back."

As the five of them crawled back behind the CATV, Nina looked around the left side of the vehicle for the driver. He lay face down in the dirt, his M12P silent, and a large gaping hole full of blood square in his back. Suddenly the shooting stopped, and the sound of charging feet came from the front of the CATV. A squad of Malerdorns had left their positions to finish Nina and the rest off. Nina was about to bring her gun around when Ngnanatuk jumped in front of her shouting, "*Mother, get down.*"

As the first couple of Malerdorns came around the right side of the vehicle, Ngnanatuk opened fire sending searing red darts into the screaming women's chests. Sipatuk and Kanapang stood up behind the CATV using it for cover and sent a barrage M12P fire into the advancing enemy. The results were deadly. The WRPs, firing from stationary positions, were much more accurate than the Malerdorns trying to fire while at a dead run. The three WRPs sent the women spinning, tumbling, screaming to the ground as red bolts of energy punched holes in their flailing bodies. Within moments it was over and nine young Malerdorn women lay dead in the valley grass, their precious blood mixing with the soil.

Fresh sounds of combat came from the valley walls along the tree line as the two marine squads (plus) hit both Malerdorn flanks. This in effect stopped all fire towards Nina and her group as the Malerdorns quickly found themselves in the defensive. Nina and the platoon leader looked at the carnage around them as the three WRPs gathered behind Nina. She looked at the lieutenant and said matter-of-factly, "This should dispel any bullshit about whether my girls will fight."

"Yes, Ma'am," the lieutenant replied sheepishly.

She turned to her WRPs, "*Daughters, today you have made me very proud; proud to be your sister.*" They smiled and nodded gently. "*Now gather your gear and let's go.*"

They had gone but a short distance along the left tree line when the shooting up ahead died. Lt. Wiggins got a status report from the squad leaders. Wiggins chuckled, "They're running off."

Ngnanatuk ran up and grabbed Nina's hand holding her back and spoke to the lieutenant. "They must stop." Wiggins stopped and looked at the young, pretty WRP. Ngnanatuk turned to Nina, "*Mother, I think the Malerdorns will return very soon, with many soldiers. We should leave this place.*"

"*Yes, Mother,*" Sipatuk and Kanapang joined in.

Nina turned to the Wiggins, "Pull your platoon back now."

"But, Ma'am, we got 'em on the run," he replied in his southern drawl.

"Pull them back now, Lieutenant!" Cpt. Errington spoke sharply.

"Aye, Ma'am," the platoon leader conceded and he called his squads to return.

Nina called the battalion TOC and informed them that they were expecting a counterattack. If that did in fact occur, they could pretty well be certain that they were on the right track. Battalion quickly ordered the remainder of Alpha Company to move to 3rd Platoon's location and be prepared to hold. Second Platoon was the closest and soon could be heard driving up the valley when suddenly the woods on the left flank and then shortly the right flank came alive with yells of charging women and the clack, clack, clack of gunfire from both sides.

Wiggins got calls from both squads that they were under heavy attack and were pulling back on the double. They couldn't help the squad in the tree line on the right, but they could help the one in front of them on the left. Nina, her three WRPs, and Wiggins formed a line from the tree line up the valley wall perpendicular to the squad's withdrawal with Nina in the middle. Wiggins called and told the squad they were waiting.

They didn't have to wait long. Shortly misdirected Malerdorn shots came zipping through the trees, pass the retreating squad, and over the heads of Nina, the platoon leader, and the three WRPs. Nina took out the two hand grenades she was carrying in a case on her hip and the others followed her lead. The number of yellow darts flying through the trees increased and the squad could be heard crushing through the scattered leaves and twigs on the ground. Almost immediately the squad could be seen and Wiggins quickly radioed them that they were right in front of his position. As soon as the squad reached Nina and the others, it spun and hit the dirt, taking up hasty positions along the line of defense. The squad leader informed the platoon leader through gasps of breath that they had lost Schneider and Clinton when they initially were hit but the charging Malerdorns.

The yells of the charging Malerdorns grew louder and louder as the hail of indiscriminately fired yellow darts grew heavier. Nina picked up a grenade, set the primer for controlled detonation, and pulled the safety pin. "Set for control detonation. Are you ready?" she called up and down the line. Everyone nodded. "Throw," she called and eighteen grenades went flying down range toward the oncoming hoard. They got back down in the prone position and watched as the screaming Malerdorns came crashing through the underbrush on line, firing hip high through the trees in front of them. "Wait for it," Cpt. Errington called. "Wait…"

Just as the company strength line of women reached the area were the armed grenades lay, Nina yelled, "Now!" and the marines and WRPs raised their remote detonators arm high in the air and squeezed the firing levers. Eighteen grenades went off almost simultaneously filling the woods with thunderous claps of explosions and razor-sharp jagged pieces of searing metal. The screaming turned horrific as the Malerdorns were carved by the merciless shrapnel. The charging line of women faltered with shock as they struggled to realize what had just happened.

But the marines and WRPs would not give them long to think about it as they opened up with a deadly line of M12P fire that cut through the women like a knife. The Malerdorns returned fire but had lost the momentum of the attack and within moments were pulling back, leaving their dead and wounded behind.

"Lieutenant, after them," Nina yelled. "Take as many prisoners as possible. Kanapang, go with them."

"Aye, Ma'am," he called. "Come on, Marines, let's move." Wiggins was quick to his feet and the squad right beside him. Although still outnumbered, the marines had the advantage at this point, chasing after a dazed and retreating enemy.

Nina stayed back with Ngnanatuk and Sipatuk and checked for survivors, disarming and administering first aid to the score of wounded. Their fighting spirit spent, the Malerdorns gratefully accepted the aid, some even chatting briefly with their WRP sisters. Ngnanatuk wept as she viewed the number of dead and wounded from a senseless, ill-led charge. Nina pulled her aside and held her for a moment.

"Are you all right, daughter?" Nina asked as she held Ngnanatuk closely.

"Why must there be so much death, Mother? Why must I watch so many of my sisters die? I hate Enitir, I hate her. I hope her skin rots off and her insides burst." Nina cringed.

The right side of the valley did not fare so well. Over half of them, around eight marines fell in the withdrawal. Fortunately, 2nd Platoon arrived in time to hit the attackers from the flank breaking up the momentum of the attack and eventually sending them scurrying for safer environs.

By mid afternoon the remainder of Alpha Company pulled into position and relieved the battered and battle weary 3rd Platoon. Thirty-seven prisoners, most of them wounded were medevacked back to the 14th Division FAH. Lt Col. Carter decided to jump the TOC to the mouth of the valley to facilitate operations. Back at Athenaburg, the good news was encouraging, and LG. Eastman ordered the deployment of the remainder of the 1st Marine Brigade, to include the 4th Tank Battalion, to the Kasing Valley (Kanapang, Sipatuk, Ngnanatuk), an acronym for the three brave WRPs that saved 3rd Platoon, Alpha Company from near annihilation twice.

Admiral Enitir was beside herself with anger. The battalion she had pulled out of the field to protect Lanatuk was down to thirty percent strength through their hasty action with a single invader platoon. This would never do. She needed to get Gen. Rotukana and her division in the war as quickly as possible. The next chance would be fortunately soon. In three days, the moons that hid her reinforcements would be in the proper position to deploy them to the south side of the Echo Mountains expediently without detection from the invaders a half continent away. But to be on the safe side, she needed a decoy.

"*Captain Agnnatuk, come in sister, and please sit down,*" Enitir said friendly, but authoritatively. "*General Rotukana and I were discussing the deployment of her division to finally rout these invaders off of Malerdorn. As you know,*" the admiral continued placing a cup of tea in front of Agnnatuk, "*we lost a good portion of the Itunguh Division when her transport was destroyed in the initial battle. Without General Itunguh to bravely lead her sisters, we have suffered defeat upon defeat with an unfortunate amount of desertion to boot.*

"*Fortunately we have the complete Rotukana Division waiting to descend on Malerdorn and accomplish its mission.*" Enitir nodded her head in the direction of the general as she took a sip of tea. "*The moons are, however, a great distant away and we don't want to lose any of the division in their descent here, do we?*"

Agnnatuk could feel her stomach knotting up as she waited for the hammer to drop.

"*We need a diversion; something to draw away any enemy that might be in the area, and that's where you come in.*" Enitir quickly took another sip of tea. "*As my second, I want you to take a portion of the fleet out to draw attention away from the moons. When the invaders make chase, I want you to destroy as many of these ruthless cowards as you can before returning to base.*" Enitir placed her tea down and added nonchalantly, "*Don't take out too much of the fleet. We will surely require some of it at a later date.*"

Agnnatuk stared at her classmate in disbelief. "*You would send me and a portion of your fleet to our deaths while you sit here swilling tea?*"

"*Really, sister,*" Enitir said indignantly. "*Don't tell me you would turn tail and run like the others.*"

Agnnatuk bolted up, sending her chair falling backwards. "*How dare you compare me to a coward? It is not cowardice that turns our sisters to the invaders. It is your reckless plans that demonstrate safety for no one but yourself.*"

"*Mind your tongue, daughter,*" Enitir shouted as she jumped to her feet. "*Or I'll have you in chains.*"

"*Hah!*" Agnnatuk countered. "*Go ahead; I'll live longer that way anyhow.*"

"*Be on the next flight up and prepare your mission!*" Enitir shouted as Agnnatuk stormed out of the room. She then turned to Gen. Rotukana and said dismissingly, "*That went rather well, don't you think?*"

In stealth mode, the Malerdorn space bus cleared Hera's gravitational field and streaked towards the first moon. Capt. Agnnatuk sat defiantly with her arms crossed until she felt herself become weightless and begin to float off the seat restrained only by her seatbelt. She let out a sigh and lowered her arms in resignation. It's hard to look defiant when you are floating around like a carnival balloon.

She turned and looked back at Malerdorn through the space bus window. It would have been a nice place to grow old she thought to herself. And she really would've liked to try this mating experience with a real man. She turned her head and looked out into deep space. She liked space; space was nice and for all its extremes, any one of which could be fatal, she found space free and undemanding. As they drew closer to the moon, she marveled at its bleak beauty. So much of space was that way, barren beauty, unadorned; like a young woman's breast; so beautiful that even the most elegant of trappings do nothing for it, only hide it from view.

Agnnatuk reached up and gently rubbed her breast. Even through the material of her uniform she could feel the sensitivity of her nipple. She wondered what it would be like for a man to touch her, hold her, and caress her. Listening to her sisters on Malerdorn who had experienced it, she imagined it would be wonderful. But instead she was sending herself to her death just so Enitir could fulfill her self-centered ambitions. Agnnatuk lowered her hand from her breast. She would not dwell on that now; she had her mission to prepare.

As the space bus rounded the moon, the Miurruk fleet came into view. It was a noble fleet, though still in its infancy. The Miurruks had never warred until the invaders came, so there was never any call for a large standing fleet or army for that matter. But because of the paranoia of the fathers, Miurruk now had both. Because it was so young and inexperienced, it did not fare well against this warrior race of invaders and many wonderful and beautiful sisters had been lost to these war wolves.

'War wolves.' Yet in the arms of these 'war wolves' sisters were finding love and pleasure. So much so that sister would even turn on sister for a man. Not that that didn't happen on Miurruk when two sisters became involved and another one entered the picture. But for many sisters intimate relationships with one another didn't feel right; as though there was something always missing. The relationships with men felt more natural, she was told. And even Agnnatuk admitted that something stirred within her loins and her nether region whenever she gazed upon a man. She shook her head violently. The mission. She must concentrate on the mission and stop lapsing into these distracting thoughts. Men! Such a nuisance.

Capt. Agnnatuk boarded the battle cruiser, *Rungnang*, and called all the fleet's Captains to a meeting. When they had all gathered she presented a slate from Adm. Enitir bearing her orders to take charge of the fleet and prepare a portion there of to create a diversion so that the Rotukana Division could deploy to Malerdorn. Then she presented her plan with a lengthy explanation as the reason she chose this course of action.

She spoke of the growing strength of the invaders' forces and their skill of warfare. She spoke of battles and sisters' lives spent. She spoke of sisters finding happiness with these invaders, both crossovers as well as Malerdorns. She spoke of a wonderful place where the sisters could dwell without the clutch of the slavery from the fathers. Capt. Agnnatuk put it all the best way she knew how, and told her captains what she intended to do help bring peace to the sisters of Malerdorn. In order for her plan to work properly, she would require most of the ships, if not all, in the fleet. Then, because of the danger of the mission, she informed her captains that she only wanted volunteers. No one would be forced to do what she was about to do. Even on the battle cruiser, *Rungnang*, she only wanted officers and sisters who were willing, without hesitation or remorse, to follow her on her course. Those who chose not to go would be transferred to the transports. The Captains were to go back to their officers and crews, inform them of Agnnatuk's plan and why she chose that course and that would decide how many vessels would join her on her fateful mission.

Capt. Agnnatuk did not have to wait long for the replies. To the ship, every ship in the fleet save the transports which were full of deploying troops fell in with the captain and her plan. Although it was dangerous, considering the alternatives, it made sense to the officers and crews to put everything on the line for the sake of all sisters and their peaceful existence on Malerdorn. Perhaps many would not understand their course, but that is always the case. In their hearts they knew they were right; for the sake of Malerdorn, for the breakaway from Miurruk, and for the future of all sisters.

CHAPTER THIRTEEN

Aboard the Earth ship *Singapore*, the watch officer was going about her regular duties when the proximity warning went off. She looked on the scope with widening eyes and then ran to the window. "*Nanda*...?" she gasped in her native Japanese. She grabbed the on-ship communicator.

"Admiral Rodriguez? Captain Becker? This is the watch officer, Ensign Fukuyama. Sir, Ma'am? It's the Miurruks. You've really got to come to the bridge and see this."

Rodriguez and Becker rushed from their cabins and joined the watch crew on the bridge. When they reached the window, Rodriguez exclaimed, "What the hell?"

"Oh my God," Rita Becker gasped. "It's beautiful."

"Yeah, well maybe," Rodriguez admitted. "But what the hell are they doing?"

"Having a parade?" Ensign Fukuyama offered.

Out the window could be seen the entire Miurruk forces obliquely approaching, dead slow with every external light on and every porthole unshuttered to produce more lights. Each of the dozen vessels were lit up like Christmas trees and looked like floats in a Thanksgiving parade.

"What'll we do?" Ensign Fukuyama asked, running her fingers through her short dark brown hair.

"Turn on our running lights," Rodriguez said not taking his eyes of the brilliant spectacle.

"Sir?" Fukuyama asked for confirmation. Rita, too, turned her head, mouth slightly agape, and stared at the admiral.

"Well it's obvious that they want us to see them," he said turning his head to look at Rita. "We know they can probably see us. Well, I want them to know that we want them to see us." He turned to the ensign. "Turn on the running lights. And get me a translator on the bridge."

"Aye, Sir."

Aboard the *Rungnang*, Capt. Agnnatuk watched as the large invader carrier switched on her lights. "*Is everyone out of the midship areas?*" she asked the *Rungnang*'s captain. "*They always aim amidship.*"

"*Yes, Mother,*" the captain acknowledged. "*And all hatches are secured.*"

"*Good, sister. I pray this works.*"

Lieut. Hans Zimmermann and his flight shot from the *Singapore*'s flight deck like a rocket as they soared out to intercept the Miurruk fleet. Strapped beneath their wings were the deadly torpedoes that had destroyed the Miurruk carriers leaving the Malerdorns without fighter support in space. As they neared the brightly lit fleet, Zimmermann warned his flight to watch out for any tricks to which the aliens might resort. Any moment he expected a barrage of the deadly yellow bolts to come flying their way, but none came.

Even as they were well within range of the fleet, the aliens made no move, one way or the other, to evade or assault. The *Singapore* directed Black-bat one-one to put a couple of bursts of cannon fire across the battle cruiser's bow. Hans Zimmermann responded with a burst of red darts soaring over the front section of the *Rungnang*.

Nothing happened. He tried another burst and watched as the red bolts of energy disappeared harmlessly out into space. Again no response came from the aliens; not one yellow dart of radiation. Zimmermann flew his deadly Hellcat up along side of the Rungnang for a closer look. In almost every window or porthole, he saw Malerdorn women in their dress uniforms with their hands raised above their heads.

"*Singapore*, this is Black-bat one-one, over."

"This is the *Singapore*."

"This is black-bat one-one. I do believe these ladies mean to surrender, over."

Aboard the Singapore, Rodriguez stared out the window for a few moments before turning to Rita Becker. "Okay, Rita, I'll bring the *Hiroshima*, the *Saõ Paulo*, and the *Boston* slowly around in case the Malerdorns change their minds. You start sending over shuttles to get those women off as quickly as you can. Be sure they are searched and when a ship is reportedly empty, send in teams to search for weapons, explosives, and stragglers."

"Aye, Sir."

"Then I'll get with III Corps and let them know they got a shit load of prisoners coming."

It took hours to clear all twelve vessels of prisoners and search the vessels for booby traps, explosives and stragglers. The prisoners were then shuttled down to the already occupied PW camps. But this load of prisoners was too much, so construction began immediately on more hasty PW compounds.

The Miurruk fleet was secured and moored together and left in a safe orbit around Hera. They could be used as warships at a later date by the Race or dismantled for parts. Either way, their existence was recognized as very useful by III Intergalactic Corps.

On the other side of the planet, the Rotukana Division was safely deployed undetected and without incident to the south side of the Echo Mountains where they could be immediately brought into combat.

Capt. Agnnatuk had successfully done her job. She diverted the invader fleet without a single loss of a sister's life. Although she lost the fleet to the invaders, she figured that would have happened anyway if they had attacked with no appreciable loss to the invaders' fleet and much loss of life for her and her sisters. Besides, she knew it would take more time to clear the ships of prisoners and process them for movement down to the PW camps than to blow up the ships. This way she bought even more time for the Rotukana Division to deploy.

Some might consider her a coward or a traitor for capitulating the fleet, but she didn't care. Agnnatuk knew in her heart she had done it right and she had the backing of every officer and sister who volunteered for the mission. As she boarded the shuttle to be ferried down to the PW camps, Agnnatuk smiled to herself. She wasn't too old and still attractive. There might still be a chance yet for her to capture one of these handsome invaders for herself.

Admiral Enitir exploded in rage when she heard the reports. "*How could she, that traitor woman? How could she surrender the entire fleet without as much as a shot?*"

"*She did what you asked,*" Gen. Rotukana defended. "*She bought us time to move the entire division down undetected; more than enough time. Pretty clever, I think. It takes more time to capture someone than to shoot her. Besides, I understand the invaders treat prisoners well. Perhaps that's why it was reported that every officer and sister that went with her volunteered.*"

"*How can you defend her?*" Enitir continued untouched by the general's words. "*She lost us the fleet. What influence can we now wield in space?*"

"*You are shortsighted, sister,*" Rotukana countered in her calm by dominating way. "*The fleet could have been lost if it had gone into a full fight with the invaders. You said yourself how strong they were. We don't even have air cover up there. Their fighters would have been all over the fleet like insects at a picnic. Agnnatuk did not lose the fleet; she just lent it to them. The fleet is safe and sound orbiting Malerdorn. And the crews. The crews aren't dead floating away in space. They are being well cared for until we break them out.*

"You want to go back to Miurruk and free our sisters. Well, your fleet is waiting for you. After we win the ground war, we'll just go and take it back."

Adm. Enitir sat slowly in her chair looking out into the distance as she visualized the words coming from Rotukana's ripe full lips. *"Yes, yes,"* she whispered as Rotukana exposed the other side of the coin. When the general had finished, Enitir sat up alert and turned her head squarely like a puppet towards Rotukana and shouted excitedly, *"Maybe I should give her a medal."*

To move a whole infantry division, even under the best of stealth, without detection is very difficult especially if it has some heavy equipment like howitzers, which are particularly necessary in mountain warfare, and large antiaircraft pieces. It did not take III Intergalactic Corps long to discover the division as it moved through the mountain passes north towards the 1st Marine Brigade. Satellite imagery painted a frightening picture, especially to the marines at the mouth of Kasing Valley.

III Corps was reluctant to commit any more forces to the Echo Mountains because of the enemy threat that remained around Athenaburg. Especially for the sake of the civilian population, Athenaburg must remain secure. It didn't make sense. A couple of enemy battalions applying unconventional warfare were tying up an entire infantry division leaving a marine brigade to slug it out with an enemy infantry division (plus). With these odds and considering the mountainous terrain, the 1st Marine Brigade could never generate enough combat power to rout an infantry division, much less one possessing heavy artillery.

LG. Eastman decided to finally meet the enemy face to face, so he requested that the senior most PW be brought to his office with a translator. Shortly the corps translator, Turrigan, entered with Capt. Agnnatuk decked out in her dress uniform of white with blue and silver trim. Eastman found Agnnatuk stunning, a woman in her late forties with ash blond hair and large blue eyes. She had a long straight nose and thin red lips that smiled from ear to ear when they were introduced. She stood tall, her shoulders back and dignified. When she sat in the chair she was offered, Agnnatuk sat erect with her back straight, her legs curled under her, and her hands resting one on top of the other on her lap.

Eastman got a hold of himself, slightly shaking his head and offered, "Would you like some coffee?"

Turrigan translated and then gave Agnnatuk's response. "She doesn't know what coffee is, but she said she would have whatever the General is having."

Eastman ordered up some coffee and cream and sugar just in case. The coffee came and Turrigan helped serve. Agnnatuk looked gently into Turrigan's eyes and spoke slowly and distinctly.

"She says it's bitter," Turrigan explained.

"Offer her some sugar," Eastman suggested.

Turrigan did as instructed. "She says it's much better," Turrigan smiled.

With the coffee just right, Eastman started off with some general questions about her health and her treatment in the PW camp. Agnnatuk replied that she had no complaints. He asked her about her home and family and did she miss Miurruk. Bob Eastman found her voice fascinating even though he could not understand one word. He didn't bother with questions like personnel strength, unit movements, or anything like that. Those had been asked by Col. Ng's people and he had already read the reports. Now he was more interested in finding out about the woman.

"Why did you surrender your fleet?"

Turrigan translated the question and Bob listened carefully to her voice as she lightly spoke her response.

"The Captain did not want to see any more of her sisters die," Turrigan replied.

"What can I do to end this bloodshed?" Eastman asked sincerely.

Agnnatuk's voice sang lightly through the air and echoed softly in Eastman's ears. He closed his eyes halfway in an effort to pick up the lilt and rhythm of her words.

"If it were up to the Captain, hostilities would have ceased months ago. There's nothing the General can do. Until Admiral Enitir is stopped, conflict will endure."

Eastman already knew what Enitir wanted; the whole damn planet. That would not work. He looked Agnnatuk straight in the eyes and with some hesitation, because he suddenly found himself not wanting to lose her, offered the Captain her freedom. "If I allow you to return to the Malerdorns, would you offer my sincere hope to Enitir that we might coexist on this planet?"

Turrigan translated and Agnnatuk looked him straight in the eyes for a moment and then down at her hands. She spoke quietly but audibly, slowly and without force.

"Captain Agnnatuk says she cannot return to the Malerdorns. She would be put to death for surrendering the fleet. She along with all the officers and crew are potential crossovers, otherwise they would not have made this leap of faith into the arms of their enemies. She does not want to go back. She understands her sisters here are happy and respected; not slaves. She wishes to stay with the Herans.

"The Captain also says that Enitir would never share the planet. It has already been suggested to her by her own sisters. She says for there to be peace, Admiral Enitir must leave."

Eastman sat back in his chair. War seemed to be the rut the infant history of humankind on Hera was stuck in. He turned his attention back to Agnnatuk. "She wants to cross over?"

Turrigan reconfirmed with the Malerdorn captain.

"What reassurances do I have that she is sincere and not using a ploy?" Eastman asked afraid of jumping to quickly.

Again Turrigan brought the General's question to her. Agnnatuk looked in his eyes understanding his doubt. What could she say that would convince him of her sincerity; nothing. Finally she touched her fingertips to her heart. "*The women of Miurruk have already learned a lot from you invaders, the people of Heran. We have learned of love, family, lives spent together with one another, supporting one another, loving one another. We have seen it in the prisoners we've taken. Never have we seen such love.*

"*I am a woman. I am forty-nine years old, my days march forward relentlessly. I will never grow younger. I want that life, I want it now. I want to find someone who can love me and, if possible, give me a child. I want a family and a home. These things I can never have on Miurruk; these things I will never have in Enitir's world. I beg you, General, please give me that chance. Allow me to cross over. I swear on my mother's blood, I will never betray your trust.*"

Eastman listened to Agnnatuk's pleading words and to Turrigan's translation. He sat for a moment absorbing the words and their meaning like taste testing a glass of wine. "John," he called suddenly.

"Yes, Sir," he answered sharply.

"Get me Col. Ng, ASAP, John."

"Yes, Sir."

Moments later, Col. Ng came running into the door. "Yes, Sir?" she panted lightly.

"Lilly," Bob Eastman began. "This is Captain Agnnatuk."

"Yes, Sir, we've met."

"I want her placed under house arrest."

Lilly stopped breathing and stared at the general. "Sir. She's already a prisoner of war."

"I know that, Lilly," Bob motioned with his hands. "I don't want her incarceration tightened; I want it lightened."

"Ahhh," Lilly nodded.

"Put her in the field grade officer quarters with a door guard."

"Yes, Sir."

"She's crossing over. Have someone take her downtown and buy her a couple of dresses. I want her out of the uniform today."

"And the bill?"

"I'll pay."

Lilly smiled. "And will you be paying for all the crossovers' dresses, Sir?"

"Lilly!" Bob snapped back good heartedly. "And set her up for intensive English lessons starting tomorrow." He thought for a moment, and then scratched his head nervously. He turned to Turrigan and said softly, "Ask the Captain if she will join me for dinner tonight."

Lilly puckered her lips with tongue in cheek and nodded slowly to herself her eyes sliding to the right as Turrigan posed the question.

"Yes, Sir," Turrigan replied. "She would be honored to."

"And have them set an extra; uh, two extra places at my table tonight for dinner."

"Two?" Lilly asked biting her lower lip.

"Well, one for the translator," Bob shrugged sheepishly.

"Of course. Anything else, Sir?" Lilly said as she pushed her lower jaw down with her tongue, making small jerks with her head from side to side.

"No, Lilly. And why are you doing this to me?"

"Jealousy, pure unadulterated jealousy," Ng said as she took Capt. Agnnatuk in tow and turned and walked down the hall; her voice fading, but the words ringing out clearly. "You never buy me dresses or post guards by my door or give me English lessons or invite me to sit by you at the dinner table …."

The reports kept coming in as Lt Col. Carter and Maj. Errington studied the map. A division-size element was pouring into the mountains, branching out to go around various peaks, never permitting themselves to bottleneck, and never allowing themselves to lose momentum.

"Either they've gotten smarter over the past couple of months or they've gotten themselves a new commander on the ground," Ben said as he lightly scratched the nape of his neck.

"I suspect the latter," Glenda said matter-of-factly. "This is going to get dicey. Any more word yet from Brigade?"

"Not since the last report," Ben shrugged. "We're still expecting air support, but as for ground units, the 1st Brigade is on its own."

"Scared?"

"Wouldn't be if John Wayne and Arnold Schwarzenegger were here."

"Who?" Glenda asked taking her eyes of the map and turning towards Ben.

Ben just shook his head, "Ghost from the past; long past. Ma'am, they have at least a three to one advantage. They have the high ground. They have heavy artillery, and as far as we know, they still have air. Aren't we pushing our luck a little bit here?"

"Ben, not since your time have the Marines faced such a challenge. Even during the Martian Revolution we were always the superior force."

"How did they win, then?"

"C.O.P.E. doesn't like killing people. They always search for the peaceful solution. In the Martians' case it was secession. Anyway, we are not totally without advantage. Our soldiers are seasoned; baptized and honed in combat. Theirs are all rookies fighting for a planet that is not even theirs. We cannot return so easily; Hera is our home. Our equipment is better and I would put the mettle of any of my marines up to any of their soldiers any day of the week. Besides," she said as she pulled the dog tag chain around her neck out from her blouse, and dangled the Episcopal service cross hanging along side her dog tags for Ben to see. "I have all the luck I need." As Glenda stuffed the chain back into her blouse, she turned and headed for her office. "Keep me posted," she said as she departed.

Ben turned to his Assistant S3, "I didn't know the Colonel was religious."

The captain looked surprised. "You aren't, Sir?"

Now Ben was surprised. "You are?"

The captain pulled out his dog tag chain exposing his Jewish service Star of David. Ben nodded his head. He was ashamed of himself. He hadn't realized how little he knew his own comrades.

For two days the division moved through the valleys and passes of the mountains. Drones sent over to reconnoiter were blasted from the sky in turn by the Malerdorns' sophisticated air defense weapons. III Intergalactic Corps was not prepared to send its precious few fighters out on reconnaissance, so it ended up having to rely on satellite imagery to track the Malerdorn division's advance through the rugged mountains.

Ben hardly slept as he watched the movement on the map of the Malerdorn forces drawing ever closer. He conferred with Glenda, the company commanders, and the brigade S3. They were not in a position to attack, and III Corps did not want to give up the Kasing Valley. Although tactically unimportant; politically, and therefore strategically, it was a message to the Malerdorns that the Herans were there to stay. This was the side of war that Ben hated most. Politics. Good men and women dying so those in power could prove a point. He shook his head. In all the advancements humankind had made over the eons, the poison of partisan politics still polarized people's persuasions.

Ben met aside with Nina whenever they could find the opportunity. He was so afraid of losing her. He had not been this worried since their initial descend onto the planet. Time seemed never so much against them as it did now. The precious moments they could lie in each other's arms were few and never long enough. Ben tried to prepare himself for that fateful day when the dogs of war would forever rend them apart, but he couldn't. He tried to consider himself lucky and thought about the countless families in history destroyed and torn apart by war; but he couldn't. When it happens to oneself, one always feels that he got the worse deal.

Gen. Rotukana entered Adm. Enitir's office as directed. "*How goes it, sister?*" Enitir started as soon as she saw Rotukana. "*How progresses your division's deployment?*"

"It goes very well, sister," Rotukana answered. *"And my scouts report that the enemy unit at the base of the valley grows no stronger."*

"They have either overestimated their capability or underestimated your strength," Enitir chuckled. *"When will you be ready to attack?"*

"The morning after next," Rotukana announced confidently.

"And the air defense units," Enitir asked excitedly. *"How goes it with them?"*

"Excellent, sister. They have knocked out everything that has dared passed overhead."

By the evening of the following day, Rotukana's troops were in place and rested before the next day's push to drive the invaders out of the mountains and off of Malerdorn. The artillery was rolled into positions under cover of the sophisticated camouflage to provide indirect fire over the hills and mountains for the advancing Rotukana Division. Antiaircraft batteries were positioned around the mountain ranges to provide direct fire against any incoming aircraft. Rotukana was in her field division headquarters reviewing the next day attack with her brigade commanders. Everyone was very confident and morale soared. The Rotukana Division was ready. The next day would decide the fate of the sisters and Malerdorn.

CHAPTER FOURTEEN

It rained all that night bringing an icy chill on the ghostly fog that choked the valley. It was reported that snow was falling in the higher elevations and there was a danger of creeks rising out of their banks. Ben pitied the troops out in this cold wet weather, trying to keep alert and warm and dry, at the same time. All night he listened to the rain hitting the top of the TOC; sometimes so loud he couldn't hear the person next to him. He even wondered how the Malerdorns were faring in this inclement weather. They were at higher elevations still, so they must be cold, he thought. Maybe they'll get cold, wet, and tired and go home.

He finally turned his station over to the assistant S3 and went to his tent. Nina was inside and had already turned in and wrapped herself in blankets against the cold. Ben got undressed and crawled in beside her, snuggling up against her warm body. He curled up behind her and slid his hand underneath her tee-shirt and cupped her breast. She wiggled and nestled as close to him as she could and they both drifted off to sleep.

A few hours later a marine was sent to awaken Maj. Errington; the Malerdorns were on the move. Ben rolled out of his dry, warm blankets to a cold and dank morning. He quickly dressed and ran to the TOC. Satellite imagery showed the Malerdorns moving across the entire front. 1st Battalion would be the first to be hit; it was the deepest in the Kasing Valley. Directly behind them to the east, 2nd Battalion had set up secondary defensive positions in the event 1st Battalion couldn't hold. 2nd Battalion was also in a position to reinforce the 1st Battalion lines if need be. 3rd Battalion lay to the northeast protecting the brigade's right flank and forming a ready reserve. The 4th Tank Battalion had attached a tank company each to 2nd and 3rd Battalions with its 3rd Tank Company being held in reserve near the brigade TOC.

The Kasing Valley was a narrow valley that ran between two large mountains; Penelope Peak to the north and Mount Hermes to the south. Between the two mountains, on the right side of the valley, stood a lesser peak, Pan. Pan commanded the best view of the valley through almost its entire length, especially the narrowest and steepest part of the valley known as Kasing's Throat. Pan was occupied by Charlie Company, 1st Battalion.

The rest of the battalion was situated east of Pan with Alpha Company on the left and Bravo Company on the right. Anything coming through Kasing's Throat had to go through them. The mountainsides of Penelope Peak and Mount Hermes were rough and in places steep making their traversal slow and tedious. If an attack were to come from this part of the Echo Mountains, it would most probably come down Kasing Valley.

Unfortunately, due to the hasty occupation of the 1st Marine Brigade at the mouth of the Kasing Valley, long range patrols had not yet been sent out, so the brigade along with 1st Battalion were relying on satellite imagery for most of their terrain analysis. The imagery showed objects down to the size of one meter because of vehicle constraints, but what was impassable for vehicles was not necessarily impassable for ground soldiers. To the west of Pan and northwest of Mount Hermes, the valley flattened out above Kasing's Throat. Although strewn with large boulders and etched with gullies, this terrain was in fact passable for the foot soldier however laborious.

This is exactly what Gen. Rotukana had planned. While the 1st Marine Brigade was huddled up against the rain, her troops had spent the night trudging through the mud, jumping over small rain-filled streams, and splashing through puddles. In fact, for Rotukana, the rain was a godsend; it masked the advancement of her troops over the relatively flat, boulder-strewn dale west of Pan and northwest of Mount Hermes in what would come to be called The Rotukana Approaches. The movement that satellite imagery was observing was from vehicles mostly. The satellite was not capable of detecting the movement of individual soldiers from its altitude high above Hera.

She set her heavy artillery at the northern side of a high, steep ridge known as The Wall. From there her artillery fire could easily clear her troops on The Rotukana Approaches and target the 1st Battalion's defensive positions. Her air defenses were set up on the high ground overlooking her artillery, her advancing forces, and Lanatuk.

She would attack with one of her brigades to clear the enemy in the valley. This would clear the narrow passage (Kasing's Throat) for the rest of the division to pour through and out onto the open valley floor where it could deploy on a wider front to rout the remainder of the enemy forces. After that, she would be in a position to easily maneuver against the enemy invaders at Athenaburg.

It was just before sunrise; that time of the early morning hours when the sky lightens fading the stars to nothing and slowly brings color back onto the blackened landscape. Ben stepped outside the TOC for a breath of fresh air and a good stretch. The rain was long gone with the clouds that brought it; it looked like a promising day of good weather. The air was crisp and clean and he could see Pan, three kilometers away, silhouetted against the brightening sky. He was wondering how Charlie Company was faring up there in the cool morning air when bright flashes of light suddenly began to sparkle all over Pan's southern face. The air around the surface appeared to get darker and darker as the small flashes continued in the quiet of the morning.

A head popped out from behind the TOC flap. "Sir! Charlie Company's under attack," and disappeared back inside again.

Astounded, Ben turned back around and looked back at Pan as more and more flashes lit up the mountainside. Then he heard the distant booms of the first flashes he had seen ten seconds earlier. Artillery! At a little over three kilometers away, it took almost ten seconds for the sound waves to reach the TOC area. Now the distant rumbling of artillery was constant. Ben turned and ran into the TOC. The place was jumping to life as reports were coming in from Charlie Company, who was under a heavy artillery cannonade, and from the other companies reporting what they were seeing. Ben got on the radio with the company commander, Cpt. Karl Meyers, who could only report that they were under a heavy attack with no word yet on casualties.

"Ben?" Lt Col. Carter called as she poked her head inside the tent. He turned and she motioned with her head to join her outside. Maj. Errington told his operations staff that he would be right back and he turned to join the commander.

When he got outside, Glenda Carter was watching the artillery pound Pan. "What's the report?" she asked calmly.

"Karl Meyers only said that they were under heavy fire from artillery and he didn't have any word on casualties."

Glenda nodded as she continued to watch. "Alpha and Bravo Companies are aware?"

"Yes, Ma'am."

She nodded again as she squinted her eyes and pouted her lips in deep thought as she stared at the cannonade on Pan. "The Malerdorns are probably trying to sneak forces through Kasing's Throat. It would take a long time to get a division through that narrow passage; after all it's only five hundred meters wide at its narrowest point." She bit her lower lip as she slowly shook her head. "Ben, I wonder if we missed something."

"Like what?"

"Like another way through that valley. They're still pounding Charlie Company. I believe all hell's going to break loose as soon as the barrage stops." Glenda turned to Ben. She had absolutely no expressing on her handsome face. Her words were calm and barely audible over the distant rumbling of cannon shell impact. "Go, Ben. Alert the companies to expect an attack at anytime. Give Brigade a status report. I'll be right in."

"Aye, Ma'am." Ben returned inside the TOC and only had been a minute when the shelling stopped. He ran back outside and stood by Glenda's side. He looked up at Pan just in time to see a half a dozen boomerang fighters soar in and pound Charlie Company positions with large yellow bolts of radiation. Almost at the same time a wall of artillery fire came marching down the valley towards Alpha and Bravo Companies' positions.

Glenda turned and patted Ben on the front of his shoulder, "Let's go," and she headed into the TOC. They went straight to the map and looked at Charlie Company's positions very carefully. "There," she said pointing to the map at the area directly west of Pan. "They definitely aren't advancing up the steep walls of Kasing's Throat; they must be coming from there."

"But I thought that area was impassable," Ben said.

"Apparently not. Let's get them some air support up there."

Charlie Company had not had time to breath from the moment the last artillery shell exploded on their position spewing rocks, dirt, and shrapnel when the first of the boomerang fighters came tearing in hitting the company lines with direct fire. Pan was shaped like a pear with the smaller end pointing west. It was there that the 3rd Platoon was dug in, and it was there that the heaviest bombardment was taking place.

Third Platoon was being hit pretty hard when they reported a wave of infantry walking up the slope. Behind them another wave, and behind them, another. These Malerdorns weren't running like crazy and shooting all over the place like the ones had before. They were walking steadfast up the hill and holding their fire for a target. These were definitely a different class of Malerdorn women. They continued up the slope saving their energy while their boomerang fighters made run after run against the marines dug in on Pan. As soon as the women were well within one hundred meters of the Charlie Company positions, the fighters darted off to the southwest over the mountains and out of sight.

Third Platoon was done to half strength when they were finally able to poke their heads up out of their holes. The sight before them was terrifying; a battalion of women advancing steadily on their right flank. The platoon leader called the company commander for help as his platoon opened fire on the Malerdorns. With red darts of death coming down on them, the wave of women picked up their pace and started to return fire. Instead of firing from the hip, they would stop momentarily, take aim, squeeze off a few rounds, and then move out quickly again. This made their fire more accurate and kept the heads of the marines down more. Up and down the slope, red darts of energy exchanged places with yellow darts of energy as the distance between the two sides steadily decreased. The women of Malerdorn started yelling as they quickened the pace even more; sending blood curdling fear down the spines of the few remaining marines in the 3rd Platoon and their fire becoming more effective with each step they took.

First Platoon on the east end of Pan had received the least amount of fire, so Karl Meyers sent it around to help reinforce the third platoon. The 1st Platoon passed behind 2nd Platoon down towards the neck of the pear where 3rd Platoon had its positions when it ran smack into the advancing Malerdorns. They were too late; 3rd Platoon was effectively gone. Now 1st Platoon found itself falling back towards the top of Pan, the shear volume of fire from the advancing Malerdorns was no match for the thirty man unit as it too was being sliced up.

Second Platoon was in an ineffective position as the Malerdorn women were advancing straight up their flank. They left their fighting holes and joined the remnants of 3rd Platoon in its effort to hold back the advancing hoard, but it was of no use. There were just too many women.

Cpt. Karl Meyers called down to battalion for immediate reinforcements, but there were none to send. Alpha and Bravo Companies were now all curled up in their foxholes as artillery rained down on them. He requested permission to pull back. Battalion granted him permission to withdraw, but he was told not to head east, the most direct route back to battalion because he would run into enemy artillery and might be mistaken for the enemy by Bravo Company and receive friendly fire. He was instead told to go northeast along the contour line of the slope until he was behind the battalion and come in from the rear.

By now 2nd and 3rd Platoons were all intermixed as they fought their way back through the company CP area and around the top of Pan. Along the southern face of Penelope Peak they withdrew as the Malerdorns kept their pace steady and their aim true. One by one, marines tumbled or were thrown on the ground by the devastating fire of the advancing infantrywomen. The marines returning fire also left its mark as they left one dead or dying Malerdorn woman after another on the ground to be stepped over by her charging sisters. As they entered the tree line along the southern face of the mountain, the shooting stopped. The remainder of Charlie Company, about twenty-two tired and discouraged Marine men and women, some wounded, dragged themselves around the contour of Penelope Peak as the victorious cheers of the Malerdorns could be heard roaring off of Pan. Cpt. Meyers paused and looked at his disheartened marines as they walked, heads down, around the contour of the slope to get behind the battalion. It was a sad day for Charlie Company,

1st Battalion, 1st Marine Brigade; they had left almost four-fifths of their comrades on Pan.

Back on Pan, the Malerdorn battalion was securing its positions, preparing for a possible invader counterattack, but none was forthcoming. The women of Malerdorn tended to the wounded from both sides and gathered the handful of prisoners to be moved quickly to the rear, to Lanatuk. Finally they prepared for the next phase of their operation as they watched Alpha and Bravo Companies being hammered with artillery. To the south they could see the rest of their brigade, approximately two battalions in strength, moving with their motored vehicles through Kasing's Throat.

Ben turned to Glenda, "The Malerdorns have Pan and the high ground." Glenda nodded. "Charlie Company is combat ineffective," he continued, "and Alpha and Bravo Companies are being chewed up by artillery. Surely a ground attack will hit them next."

Glenda sighed. "Let's call the Brigade for help before it's too late."

"Aye, Ma'am."

Even as Brigade was deploying the 3rd Tank Company to reinforce 1st Battalion, the artillery fire lifted and the swarm of boomerang fighters returned to place direct fire on the embattled companies' positions. But their attack was cut short when a flight of Hellcats came screaming southwest over the foothills to engage the fighters. The boomerang fighters evaded in every direction as two were instantly destroyed and fell to earth in balls of flames. The boomerang fighters headed back to the southwest over the Kasing valley with the Hellcats in hot pursuit. But as the Hellcats flew deeper into the valley, a burst of antiaircraft fire shot up into the Hera sky like a white wall of fireworks.

One Hellcat disintegrated in midair in an orange and yellow flash. Two more headed to the ground trailing smoke and flames, crashing into the rocky mountain walls. Yet another limped back to the northeast trailing grey-white smoke in its wake. The remaining two made a wide arc around the antiaircraft infested area with boomerang fighters coming up their tails. The trailing Hellcat was able to down two of the small fighters before it was overcome by a hail of yellow darts from several others. It nosed down and disappeared behind the mountains. The sixth and final Hellcat headed back towards the northeast at full speed.

With their air cover gone, Alpha and Bravo companies again faced the onslaught of the boomerang fighters. The battalion's antiaircraft platoon was able to cope with a couple of the fighters, sending one into Mount Hermes, but they were the first targeted and soon were knocked out of action. Despite the continuous attacks by the boomerang fighters, the companies were able to see the advancing Malerdorn infantry. Driving up in heavily armed, armored personnel carriers (APC), the Malerdorns advanced quickly over the two kilometers that separated them and the defending invaders. Yellow bolts of radiation shot incessantly from the Malerdorns' APCs' cannons shredding the ground to coleslaw where they struck.

The 1st Battalion's antitank platoon struck back with anger, their large red bolts easily penetrating the APCs' armor leaving a couple of burning hulks with burning soldiers inside. The Malerdorns learning yet another lesson quickly dismounted and continued the attack on foot.

As the Malerdorns drew nearer, the battalion's mortar platoon opened up lofting shells over Alpha and Bravo Companies' positions and into the face of the enemy. Heavy mortar shells slammed into the earth, exploding in a dull flash of orange flame and black smoke, sending large chunks of shrapnel hissing through the air, hacking effortlessly through the line of advancing women.

By the time that the first wave of Malerdorn infantrywomen reached the battalion lines, it was pretty much decimated, with scores of young women lying lifeless in its wake. But they were soon joined by the second wave which pushed into the companies' lines where hand to hand fighting took place. The Malerdorns were not quite as strong as the male marines, but they greatly out numbered the marines and easily took them down with bayonet and maul.

When the 3rd Tank Company arrived, the forces were all intermixed and so the tanks could not bring the full weight of their power to bear except on the APCs in the distance. At this they were deadly, but their glory short lived as the boomerang fighters returned to give close air support. Burning tanks soon joined the burning APCs as the third wave approached the lines.

Ben was in the TOC receiving the reports. It looked pretty grim. Brigade was deploying 2nd Battalion, but they were still four kilometers to the rear. He had no idea where Nina was at that moment, only that she and her WRPs were providing support to the companies. Considering the condition the companies were in, he was very worried.

He was standing at the map talking with Glenda when suddenly the map board exploded as a bolt of yellow light zipped between them and into the board. Then another dart entered the TOC and another. One punched its way through Cpt. Mary Paxton's chest and she flew back into the wall cover of the TOC and collapsed in a heap on the floor. The inside of the TOC was sheer panic as bolts of radiation zipped through the thin flexible cover.

"Everybody out," Glenda screamed as the entire TOC seemed to be ablaze with Malerdorn fire.

Ben dropped down and crawled out from under the canvas like wall to the back of the TOC, but Glenda did not follow. He turned around and saw her lying on the TOC floor. He grabbed her by the boot and dragged her outside. She had blood coming from her chest, but not the kind of hole that a weapon makes. Ben tore open her blouse to find a piece of shrapnel lodged in her chest, just below her bra. Ben touched the large sliver of metal, but Glenda moaned with pain. At least she's alive, he thought. She opened her eyes and whispered his name.

"Ma'am," he said. "I'm afraid to move you."

"No," she whispered. "Leave me. Go find Nina."

"I'm not leaving you, Ma'am."

"Go. That's an order," she groaned.

"You can court-martial me in the morning, Ma'am. I'm not leaving you." Ben sat beside Glenda, with her head in his lap as she lay panting.

She raised her right hand to his cheek, "Nina's such a lucky woman. She's lucky to have you." Her hand dropped suddenly and her eyes shut.

"Ma'am? Ma'am?" Ben called as he grabbed her head and shook it, but she didn't answer. Suddenly Ben found himself surrounded by Malerdorn soldiers, their weapons all pointed at him.

It was over, he thought. The battalion wiped out, so many people he knew; dead. Even as the battle raged around him, explosions in the distance, the sounds of aircraft overhead and gunfire everywhere, and now perhaps he, too, would die; die so far away in time and distance from that Montana prairie where he had first met Nina.

"*Freeze, sisters, or die.*" The voice was familiar to him. "*Drop your weapons or die.*"

"*Drop your weapons, sisters, or we'll kill you all,*" came a different voice from a different direction.

"*Empty your hands, sisters. Do it now,*" came yet another voice. And the Malerdorns began laying their weapons on the ground. As they did, Nina and a bunch of her WRPs came out from hiding and surrounded the Malerdorns. Nina went immediately to Ben.

"She's dead," Ben whispered his eyes welling up in tears.

Nina pulled out a small vital signs reader from her first aid kit and placed it on Glenda's chest. Immediately the numbers began to register. "She's alive," Nina smiled.

"I thought I'd lost you. I thought I'd lost everybody," Ben choked with trembling lips as tears ran down his dirty cheeks.

Nina wiped away the tears, leaned forward, and lightly kissed him on the mouth. "I'm so lucky to have you," she smiled.

"That's what she said, that you were lucky to have me."

"See?" Nina smiled as she stood up and slung her weapon across her shoulder. "You should listen to women more often. Now let's get the Colonel a corpsman."

As the Malerdorn prisoners were being lead away, one stopped and addressed Nina. "*You speak Miurruk, but you are not one of us,*" she said.

"*That's right,*" Nina replied.

"*You are not one of us, but you called us 'sisters.' Why?*"

"*We are all sisters and brothers, sister. The sooner you learn that, the sooner we can stop killing each other.*"

2nd Battalion was well through the lines when the corpsman arrived. They had routed the Malerdorn brigade in the assault with the assistance of the rest of the 4th Tank Battalion. The *Singapore* orbiting Hera had released all of its remaining Hellcats to the fight. They realized it was sink or swim time, and now was not the time to be shy. Despite the loss of seven more Hellcats to Malerdorn antiaircraft fire, the Hellcats were eventually able to knock out the antiaircraft positions which allow them to silence the artillery and beat away the boomerang fighters. Finally, the Hellcats caught the next Malerdorn brigade moving through the Kasing's Throat and rendered it combat ineffective before it could get into the open and deploy.

Gen. Rotukana refused to commit the last of her division. She refused to send any more sisters to their deaths. Without the support of Gen. Rotukana and her forces, Adm. Enitir's dream was destroyed. The Kasing Valley Battle was costly for both sides. Enitir reluctantly began to realize that if she were ever to free her people on Miurruk, she would have to preserve her precious resources on Malerdorn, mainly her sisters. Enitir sued for peace, with conditions. Although LG. Eastman could have militarily pressed for an unconditional surrender, he agreed to listen to the terms.

Enitir informed III Intergalactic Corps of her sisters' plight on Miurruk and of her plans to one day liberate her sisters from the fathers. With that in mind, she pressed for the return of her fleet with the assurance that it would never take aggressive action or assist any other entity to take aggressive action against any C.O.P.E. vessel. She requested the return of all prisoners under the assurance that all people of Hera or Malerdorn have the right to choose where and with whom they wanted to live and that she would never press any Malerdorn or Heran into service and would guarantee the right of people to choose their own fate. She also guaranteed that no punitive actions would be taken against crossovers. She asked that no charges be brought against her or any other Malerdorn for the abduction and treatment of prisoners, both military and civilian, during the war. And finally, she asked that the land from the mountains to the Southbend River to the West Sea be set aside exclusively for Malerdorns and Malerdorn administration. In other words, the Malerdorns would have their own state.

Bob Eastman wanted clearance through 5th Frontier Fleet, but since he was the commander on the ground and most aware of the situation, they left the final decision up to him. Eastman agreed to the terms and four days after hostilities had ended, a peace treaty was signed by LG. Robert Eastman and Interim Mayor Sean O'Leary on the side of the Herans and Adm. Enitir and Gen. Rotukana on the side of the Malerdorns. A large ceremony was conducted at the new Athenaburg City Auditorium with a special request by the Malerdorns that Maj. and Cpt. Errington be present. The ceremony was formal, but not too lengthy with speeches given by both sides expressing their sincere desire for peace and communion with each other.

At the end of the ceremony, Adm. Enitir requested Maj. and Cpt. Errington on the stage. Ben and Nina went up center stage with the signers of the peace accord. Adm. Enitir motioned off stage and the Malerdorn doctor, the one whom Ben had seen untie Nina from the gurney, walked up to them with a bundle nestled carefully in her arms and a smile on her face and handed it to Nina. It was her healthy baby boy taken from her many months prior.

EPILOGUE

Life became productive on Hera with both the Herans and the Malerdorns striving to build their homes. The boundary established around the State of Malerdorn was a transparent one with people from both sides visiting the other often sociably as well as in commerce. Many men from Hera married many of the beautiful Malerdorns, settled on both sides of the border, and closing even further the differences that existed between the two races.

Ben, Nina, and their new son, Thomas Errington, did not leave Hera and return to earth as they had initially planned. Nina's close attachment with her new sisters, especially her WRPs, gave her a desire to stay and forge a new life on the virgin planet. Thomas Errington was recorded as the first baby born on Hera. He was the first true Heran. Ben and Nina became Liaison Officers in the C.O.P.E. Embassy under the new Director Robert Eastman who also chose to stay and form a new life with Agnnatuk.

The rest of the convoys arrived safely and on schedule as Hera blossomed into a new industrialized civilization. Enitir continued her dream of freeing her people from Miurruk and pushed her agenda whenever she could. Gen. Rotukana remained head of the Malerdorn military and trained her volunteers for the faithful day when they would depart for Miurruk to free the remainder of their sisters.

The Hera wars marked the beginning of a new civilization on a planet fought for by its would-be inhabitants. A violent beginning for two races wishing to be free, Hera cost the Race five thousand seven hundred and twelve lives and the Malerdorns over fifty-three thousand lives. But the blood that was spilt on Hera ensured its value to two nations who swore they would never forget nor let their children forget what dear a price their home was bought.

Glossary

Adm. admiral.

ASAP as soon as possible, pronounced ā-săp.

BDA battle damage assessment.

BG. brigadier general.

Capt./Cpt. captain.

CATV combat, all-terrain vehicle, pronounced cat-vee. A small, fast, all-terrain, tracked utility behicle.

Cmdr. commander.

CMPV combat, multi-purpose vehicle, pronounced comp-vee. An eight-wheeled cargo carrier joined in three places allowing each pair of wheels to support its own section providing the vehicle excellent terrain negotiation capabilities along practically any uneven surface. Also swim capable.

Col. colonel.

Commo check communication's check.

Comms communication.

C.O.P.E. confederation of planet earth, the world body governing all the nations on earth and maintaining the world's defensive forces.

CP command post.

FAH field army hospital.

Heran an immigrant to Hera from the planet earth, anyone born on the planet Hera.

K kilometer.

Lanatuk the Miurruk hideaway city in the Echo Mountains known to the Herans as Pan.

LG. lieutenant general.

Lieut./Lt. lieutenant.

Lt Col./Ltc. lieutenant colonel.

LRRP long range reconnaissance patrol.

Maj. major.

Malerdorn the Miurruk name for Hera.

MG major general.

Mike minute as in 10 mikes or ten minutes.

Miurruk the name of the planet, people, and language of the alien women.

NCO noncommissioned officer, a corporal or sergeant.

PA physician's assistant.

SITREP situation report.

The Race anyone from planet earth, Homo sapiens sapiens.

TOC tactical operations center.